# Acknowledgments

Thank you to Anna Jensen for the Sycamore Street project and work you did to help all the authors. You are amazing.

Thank you to Amy Walsh, who invited me on this journey to Eden Cove, for reading my pages and for being a friend. P.J. Leigh, who not only reads my work, but celebrates with me on the good days and offers a shoulder to cry on for the hard days. I'm blessed to have you in my life. To my Thursday Critique Crew, Stephanie Daniels, Andra Loy, and Carrie Walker. You guys are the best.

Special thanks to Michelle Braden for her invaluable feedback.

Grateful thanks to my loves for being there. And to my readers, thank you for reading and supporting my dream!

Above all else, I am eternally thankful to the One who makes it all possible.

River Deben
Cemetery
Great Lake
Tea Garden
Town Hall
Community Center & Sports Area
Post Office
School
Lighthouse
North Sea
Eden Cove to 2024

# Chapter One

*One month before arriving in Eden Cove*

*April 1983*

In all my twenty-six years, I'd only wanted two things. One, to be with my mother again someday, and two, to make my father proud. My progress on the first task required tracking down my mother. That had stalled.

And I was completely failing on the second, going by today's lunch meeting, one Daddy had set up with a prospective business partner. In my defense, Daddy hadn't informed me of *who* the prospective business partner was. If he had, I would've voiced my opposition well before we'd been seated by the waiter.

I put my glass down onto the cream damask tablecloth and forced a brittle smile. "May I speak with you privately, Daddy?"

The clink of silverware and sedate conversations of other diners at The Point—one of Cypress Bend's finer eating establishments—continued, but the men seated at our table stilled, as frozen as an artist's tableau. *The Businessman's Folly,* they could call it, or maybe *Men About to Discuss a Bad Idea.*

No matter how intimidating Mr. Strickland was, I couldn't let Daddy make such a terrible mistake as to invest in Strickland's plan for office complexes.

Conner, Daddy's right-hand man, was doing nothing useful just now, only darting nervous glances between Daddy and Mr. Strickland. Having the appearance of the perfect realtor with his wavy hair and manly jawline didn't do Conner Harrison much good in this situation. I shot him a look, hoping he'd catch on and help me out. He pretended to be oblivious. Even though our office romance had been short-lived, Conner certainly knew me well enough to read me, but he ignored my silent plea. The rejection stung, though it wasn't completely unexpected. He tended to go along with Daddy.

I reached for my necklace, a habit when my nerves were stretched taut, and felt the cool smoothness of pearls. My key necklace was at home. I'd forgotten I'd paired the pearls with my classic navy sheath dress.

Trying not to fidget, I cleared my throat. "Daddy?"

With deliberate care, Mr. Strickland set down his knife and fork. All eyes were on the stocky man as he dabbed his mouth with his linen napkin. He smiled a wicked shark grin at me. I refused to shiver, instead acknowledging him with lowered lashes and a nod.

Dismissive, he flicked his fingers. "That's fine, Whit. Go talk with your girl."

Arrogance like his from any other man would've set my blood boiling, but I was too worried, and scared, if I told myself the truth. Daddy didn't need to partner with Strickland's kind.

## The Key Collector's Promise

Strickland's associates began eating again, and Conner took this as his cue to start telling a story about an alligator. My daddy, Bobby Whitaker Lejeune, known by all as Whit, pushed back his chair. He smoothed the front of his suit and walked toward the lobby.

All pretense of grace deserted me and, ungainly as a new colt, I hopped up and followed.

The minute we were clear of the room, Daddy spun on his heel. "What do you think you're doing?"

The power in his deep, quiet, voice took me back to childhood days when I'd gotten into trouble. Not something I'd done often.

The Shrimp Garden Salad resting uncomfortably in my belly threatened to rise, but I carried on, ignoring his tone and the way he seemed to tower over me.

There was too much at stake to be cowed.

"I could ask you the same thing! You can't seriously consider partnering with Strickland."

Daddy rubbed his temples with his long, manicured fingers. He'd worked so hard to project an image, with his well-cut suit, his stylish dark brown hair worn just short enough to avoid offending older clients, and his impeccable business dealings. Now he was throwing it all away.

Calm, and in a matter-of-fact tone, he said, "It's become necessary."

"No, it hasn't! Strickland?"

Strickland may have high connections and gave the impression he had the governor's ear, but he also had the stink of corruption clinging to him. It was well known that Strickland's company fudged safety inspections. A fact he cared not one iota about, since he wriggled out of criminal charges. It didn't keep him from having his picture in the paper. The man had a stake in every game around, from building hotels to buying up old houses at rock-bottom prices, making way for development, and making unfair profits.

Not to mention how people who stood in his way had a habit of suddenly leaving town. Rumors of payoffs and shady practices abounded.

I didn't need to know details to know we wanted no part with him.

I said, "Nothing good can come from partnering with Strickland. You can't be seriously considering this real estate deal."

Daddy glared at me, ice in his blue eyes. "The housing market is a mess. I have to think of the company's future." He lowered his brows and set his jaw in a stubborn line. "We are going back in there to talk with Mr. Strickland, and you'll behave."

At those last words, heat flushed my cheeks as if I'd been slapped. I wanted to say no, I wasn't going back in. I wanted to make him listen to reason, but he wasn't in a listening mood.

"Sandra, I know what's best." Daddy's attention moved past me and he strode away, leaving me standing alone in the lobby.

After a beat, I went along after him. What else could I do? At least this way I could keep an eye on Daddy. Through the rest of dinner, I remained silent, a perfect decorative southern woman.

As soon as we hit the parking lot, Daddy strode toward his Cutlass. I hurried after him, adding half-running hops to keep up.

"Daddy, wait. We need to talk."

Without slowing, Daddy flung his hand up and spoke over his shoulder. "I don't want to hear it, Sandra. Conner will take you home."

"Wait."

He stopped and did an about-face. Anger radiated from him, setting my skin on fire. Always hard to manage, he was never more so than when I questioned him. And I'd never questioned his business judgment before, but I had to now. Our reputation was in danger. Our livelihood. Or worse. Those who consorted with criminals tended to suffer even when innocent of wrongdoing.

I said, "Daddy, you cannot get in bed with a character like Strickland. He's a criminal."

Daddy ground out, "There's no proof."

"Do we need proof? You know his reputation. This is a bad risk."

"Listen, young lady, I think I know how to run my own business, and if you don't shut…" Nostrils flaring, he dragged in a breath.

I could almost hear him mentally counting to ten.

His left eyelid twitched, and he rubbed it. "I can't do this now."

I said, "Can we discuss it at home?"

"I don't know when I'll be in." His gaze flicked away from my face to something behind me, and I turned my head to see.

Conner. Always Conner, hovering to do Daddy's bidding. One of the reasons things hadn't worked out between us.

By the time I returned my attention to Daddy, the car's door was shut, and the brake lights glowed a red warning as he reversed.

"Come on." Conner touched my elbow, and I shrugged him off.

"You could've stopped him."

Conner's shoulders hitched the slightest bit, but he didn't utter a word; just stood there in the concrete parking lot, waiting for me to cave.

Over the next weeks, Daddy didn't budge on his position, even after I ate crow and apologized for my sin of embarrassing him, and even after I made logical objections to partnering with Strickland at every opportunity.

Staying quiet had never been my strong suit.

If I'd been less vocal or less public about my thoughts on The Strickland Project, things might've turned out differently after that.

## Chapter Two

*May 24, TUESDAY 7:30 A.M.*

On a bright, sunshiny May morning, about a month after the dinner with Strickland, I slipped my key into the front door of our office, Lejeune Realty, the top real estate company in Cypress Bend and beyond. Daddy and Conner had gone out of town on business, leaving me to open the office. The engraved sign Daddy had commissioned in better times let people know he'd made his mark in the world. It also served as a reminder that he intended for me, his only child, to continue in his steps, serving the area's real estate needs.

Such as they were these days.

What with the housing market's downhill slide, and the state of things between us, Daddy's bad humor clung to the walls of the office like freshly pasted wallpaper. I was glad he was out of pocket, giving me a much-needed breather. The proposed deadline for the Strickland deal was June 10th, and I hadn't made a lick of progress bringing Daddy around. If I could close on enough properties to get us in the black, I'd have leverage.

Daddy would have to see sense.

I turned the knob of the burnished oak door. No warning creak sounded when it swung open, no hint of danger. A puff of potpourri-scented air greeted me, a welcoming, homey fragrance meant to set clients at ease as they entered the lobby with its upholstered chairs and tasteful wall art. The toe of my navy pump almost trod on the envelope lying on the inside welcome mat in front of the rarely used brass-plated letter slot.

Bending awkwardly, I scooped up the letter, wincing at the way the waistband of my pencil skirt pinched. I carried the envelope with me to the coffee machine in the tiny break room, debating whether I should skip lunch. The extra five pounds my five-foot-seven frame carried resisted permanent banishment, and I often resorted to grapefruit and Dexatrim to keep things under control. I measured out coffee and got the machine going. Our longtime secretary, Addie, hadn't made it to the office yet.

The quiet put me off, and I tried to smother the feeling I'd been abandoned. I told myself I didn't care a fig Daddy hadn't consulted me about the trip at all yet had taken Conner along with him. In fact, Conner's absence was just another reason to celebrate a day without male opinions and so-called logic.

While waiting for the coffee, I glanced at the nondescript envelope, flipping it to read the front. Just my first name in sloppily written capital letters, nothing else.

SANDRA

How strange. Chill bumps raced up my back as I slid my index finger under the sealed flap. The letter popped open, easy as you please, as if it were an innocuous invitation to afternoon tea at the country club. Gingerly, I unfolded the paper.

The same blocky, uneven script sprawled across the white paper.

*What is your heart's desire, Sandra?*
*True love, a vacation on an island, a safe place to lay your head at night?*

A half-smile, half-frown tugged at my lips. What kind of riddle was this? I kept reading.

*Girls who talk too much lose precious things. Keep your mouth shut about the Strickland Project.*

There was more, but my hands were shaking so hard I struggled to make out the last line.

*Remember, family first.*

A wheezy breath escaped my lungs. My fingers went to the silver key I wore on a chain around my neck, gripping it tight. Precious things. Family first. Island. Heart's Desire. England.

Mother.

I turned the paper over, my eyes searching for clues about the sender, stupidly looking for… what? A signature? Although the meaning of the note was crystal clear, my jumbled thoughts strained to rearrange the words into a sensible, reasonable message.

Who could have sent this?

Anyone.

It was no secret I'd been searching for my mother. But someone else had found her first. Someone who didn't like my opposition to Daddy's shady dealings with Strickland.

The coffee machine hissed its final drip, the sound galvanizing me into action. I rushed to my small office and dropped into the chair at my desk, dragging the phone and Rolodex close. Tamping down panic, I flipped through the cards, lost my place, and started over again, scanning for Harlow Brushy, the private investigator I'd hired six months previously to locate my mother, and found his number.

An older lady answered the call, not Harlow. My blood pressure spiked. It took me a moment and an exchange of too many confused sentences to realize I'd mis-dialed. By then, I trembled so much the phone receiver knocked against my skull.

*Get it together, Sandra.*

Mumbling an apology, I disconnected and re-punched the numbers. Harlow's machine picked up.

"Harlow?" My voice wavered, sounding like a lost child. I cleared my throat and sat up straight. "Harlow, this is Sandra Lejeune." My thoughts flew scattershot. I couldn't very well tell the details of the letter on an answering machine. I said, "Something's happened. I need to meet with you. Urgently." I glanced at my watch, but the time didn't register. "Please call me back as soon as you get this message."

## Chapter Three

*May 24, TUESDAY 9:15 A.M.*

An hour and fifteen minutes later, a grumpy Harlow called back, informing me he hadn't located my mother yet, but he agreed I could come to his storefront office. I'd barely put my sedan in gear when Addie's brown Vega wheeled into the slot to my right. I gave her a quick wave and meant to tear out of the place, but her questioning glance stopped me. Addie had been a fixture at Lejeune Realty for years. More than just Daddy's secretary, she was like family. On several occasions, she'd provided cupcakes for school events and tissues for my young heartaches. Daddy had hired her straight out of secretary school and as far as I knew, during the twenty years since, she'd never considered leaving us.

I could no sooner ignore her than ignore a hungry puppy.

I hit the passenger's window down button and leaned across the seat. It took her a minute to crank her window down, which was just as well, since my instinct was to cry on her shoulder, an activity I didn't have time for. Besides, I didn't want to worry her.

Flustered, she fiddled with her newly coifed ash-blonde 'do. "What's wrong, Sandy?"

"Just a cranky client." The lie slid off my tongue like warm butter. Attempting nonchalance, I said, "You know how it is. I'll be back later." I rolled the window up and took my foot off the brake, not giving her a chance to weasel the truth out of me.

Instead of the usual twenty-five-minute drive, I made it to Harlow's office in fifteen. I hopped out of my car and, not bothering to lock it, barreled across the parking lot and through the glass door of Harlow's drab office as fast as my pencil skirt allowed. Harlow sat behind his desk, poking at a dried-out Danish pastry with a toothpick. Bleary-eyed and frowning, he blinked at me. He gave up on the Danish and sucked the toothpick.

Harlow always presented as gruff and a bit distant, but he'd come recommended. Neither his rumpled, slightly pudgy, graying appearance nor his manner had put me off at our first meeting, and it didn't now. I strode the few feet across the olive-green carpet and took a seat opposite him in a wooden banker's chair.

He sighed, conveying the weariness of all his years, and shifted the toothpick, letting it hang from the corner of his mouth. "Ms. Lejeune. I put in my reports on Fridays. It's Tuesday."

"I got a threat."

"What?" His sleepy eyes popped open.

"A threatening letter." I bit my lip. Did I need to mention Strickland? I thought not. It would put Daddy in a bad light. "You said you haven't found my mother, but someone else has."

"Someone found her and threatened her? Why?" Harlow scrubbed his face. "This sounds serious. Have you called the police?"

His question hit like a bucket of cold water. Why hadn't I called the police? Or Daddy?

Daddy had no love for my mother, giving me only the barest of information about her. She'd betrayed him. Taken me away without his knowledge.

An evil whisper wormed into my brain.

Rivals who got in Daddy's way paid a price, one way or another.

But that was only business, and this threatening letter was definitely personal. Besides, Daddy would never cause physical harm to a person, not even Mother. But Strickland might.

Then the thought struck. Were there other shady characters Daddy had approached?

I squeezed my temples. Police? No. Not when Daddy was in partnership with Strickland.

Hedging, I said, "I'm not sure the police could help. I need more information."

I told myself it was concern about Daddy's involvement with Strickland keeping me from notifying police and shoved away the fact of Daddy's feelings about Mother. Those were personal with a capital P.

My misty memories of her didn't match up with his claims she'd cheated, but I distinctly remembered asking my mother where Daddy was on that seaside vacation we'd taken, just her and me, when I was four years old. It was the last time I'd seen her, and the last time I'd seen England. Daddy had brought me back to his home in the States, banishing the British half of my heritage and replacing it with Louisiana's culture. I'd never completely forgotten my English mother, nor had I stopped missing her, but Harlow was the first PI I'd hired.

Harlow narrowed his eyes at me and removed the toothpick, tossing it into the aluminum ashtray on his desk. "Can I see the letter?"

"Will it be kept confidential?"

Harlow tipped his head to the side.

A headache bloomed above my left eye, and I rubbed the spot. "It's complicated."

Understatement.

He said, "If there's something you don't want me to know, keep it to yourself. Threatening letters are above my pay grade, anyway."

"Just tell me if you're any closer to finding her."

He pawed through a stack of manila files on his desk, selected one, and handed it over. "Six years ago she was renting a flat in Suffolk and working retail. She's bounced around a bit."

I opened the folder.

Harlow said, "As we talked about before, she's been in and out of the hospital a few times, and one nurse suggested diabetes, but I couldn't confirm."

I flipped through the papers. It contained the reports he'd given me before, plus one addition to the former addresses he'd tracked down, a short list of checked-off phone numbers, and six pages of Harlow's random chicken-scratched notes. A small offering, but the handful of hope was all I had.

"What are you going to do?" Harlow's brow creased. He looked worried.

I squared my shoulders. "Find her myself."

## The Key Collector's Promise

If I could. Sitting around waiting for disaster to strike wasn't an option. There was nothing for it except to fly over to England.

I didn't drive as fast going back to the office, never mind the ticking clock looming over my shoulder. Or maybe it was a ticking bomb. My fists tightened on the wheel.

*Think, Sandra.*

I had enough information and clues to at least start looking for my mother, and I couldn't think of any other way to continue the search, warn my mother, yet keep Daddy from the complication of a police investigation.

What kind of people was he dealing with? A shiver ran down my spine. I had to be careful and smart—just the way he'd always taught me.

I stopped by Marilynne's Bakery and ordered two éclairs, Addie's weakness. The éclairs would distract her from asking questions. My leg wiggled as I waited for the girl to stow the treats in a bag, the air so heavy with sugar I could feel the sticky molecules adhering to my skin.

It was only by sheer luck Daddy and Conner had been out of the office and I'd been the one to intercept the letter. Normally, I was the last to show up, no matter how hard I tried to get there before Conner. He liked to get one up on me, beating me to the office on Tuesdays, the only day Addie arrived after nine o'clock. She always had a hair appointment Tuesday morning.

Back in my sedan, I put the bakery bag on the passenger seat and adjusted the rearview mirror to check my face. Smeared-mascara raccoon eyes, shiny pink nose, and my shoulder-length brunette hair had morphed from curls to frizz. I looked like I'd had a hard night out and forgotten to freshen up before heading out in the morning. At least I'd brought my purse with me when I'd run out of the office. Preparing myself to wear a mask of more than one sort, I set about repairing my makeup and spraying my hair back into submission. That done, I headed for the office, rehearsing what I'd tell Addie when I got there.

I interrupted Addie's typing by placing a napkin and an éclair on her desk.

Her mouth puckered in delight. "You shouldn't have." Lifting the éclair to her lips, she inhaled and then took a bite, her eyes rolling up into her head.

My smile at her exuberance felt plastic.

Covering her mouth with her napkin, she said, "Aren't you having one?" The half-worried, half-confused expression she often wore rested on her features as she set the pastry down. She cut her eyes to the chair beside her desk, clearly expecting me to sit and enjoy a chat-and-snack session.

"Oh, sure. I'm having one." I lied, shaking the bag. No way could a morsel get past the constriction in my throat. "Mine's right here, but I have some properties to research. I'm taking it to my desk."

"Oh." Her face fell.

A dab of chocolate frosting dotting her chin made her especially winsome, and the urge to confide in her swamped me. Everything in me clamped down on that urge.

The only person Addie was more loyal to than me was Daddy, and I didn't want her calling his hotel and spilling the beans. Addie couldn't keep a secret to save her life.

I said, "It's a catch-up day for me, and I'll be working through lunch. This afternoon will be full of non-stop showings keeping me busy, but I wanted to give you a treat." Pretending

## The Key Collector's Promise

to rummage in my purse for something, I walked toward my office, went inside, and shut the door.

My immediate instinct was to book a flight for London, but then what? I needed a plan.

First, I cleared the day's calendar, calling clients and leaving messages when I couldn't speak directly with them. Daddy would be livid. Probably think I was slacking. I'd figure out what to tell him later. Stomach flu? He'd never buy that. Lejeunes powered through. I'd think of something.

Fantasy properties I'd tacked on a bulletin board, listings in England I'd gathered for myself, contained useful contact information I could use now, so I gathered the clippings and stowed them in my briefcase. The file from Harlow rested alongside the papers, and I took it out. My habit of making backup copies of important papers warred with my need to keep the details on my person. Best to make copies and secure them, I decided.

At the closed door of my office, I adjusted my shoulder pads and tucked in my blouse, stood straight, and opened the door.

Addie was on the phone. I hurried to the copier, ran off duplicates of everything in the file, and carried the still-warm pages back into my office where I stuffed them into a manila folder and secured them in the bottom file drawer, locking it.

With a fake realtor-smile in place, I strode out and breezily said, "Going to check out a property. Not sure if I'll be back before five, but I'll call and pick up any messages by then."

Blushing, Addie hid a *Cosmopolitan* magazine in her lap. "All right." She picked up a pen and scribbled on a yellow legal pad as I pushed out the door.

# Chapter Four

*May 24, TUESDAY Later*

Our sprawling, two-story house sat on fifteen acres on a private road, but with easy access to I-20. No one was about the place. I parked in the garage and cut the engine. My nerves thrummed. Sweat covered my body as if it were dog days and not ridiculously pleasant weather out. I hustled inside, and the air conditioning chilled me to the bone.

It took little time to locate my passport and book the first flight to England. I'd leave before dawn for the airport.

As I packed, the key around my neck seemed to grow heavier. It was the key to the house Mother and I had stayed at during my last summer in England, a place by the sea.

The last thing she'd said to me was, *"Promise you won't lose it."*

If Daddy'd had a clue about why I kept it, no doubt he would have insisted I throw it away, but to him, it was simply one of the keys I collected. Collecting them was a habit I'd had for as long as I could remember, encouraged by him. Ever since he'd first started selling real estate, he'd given me old keys from properties after a locksmith had re-keyed the homes. Even now,

# The Key Collector's Promise

he'd occasionally bring me a unique key for no reason besides to make me smile.

My heart pinched, and I tried not to think of how he'd react when he discovered where I'd gone. He'd be angry, for sure.

Daddy and Conner weren't due back until the wee hours of the morning, at earliest. If fortune shone on me, I wouldn't cross paths with Daddy, therefore avoiding a confrontation.

A sleepless evening stretched ahead. I flipped through cable channels, stopping at the strains of a gospel song, watching a middle-aged woman with big hair sing her heart out. The lyrics reached right through the screen and prompted a yearning for the days of Vacation Bible School, and the childhood faith I'd had. The prayer line number flashed across the bottom of the screen. Thinking it couldn't hurt, I called. At first, I clung to the kind words of the woman on the phone. She asked if I wanted to make a donation and listed the acceptable credit cards. On the TV, the shiny-faced preacher came on. Flushing with shame, I hung up and clicked off the television. I didn't know how the mysteries of God worked, but was sure buying wishes from late-night TV preachers wasn't the way.

As soon as it was morning in England, I began calling estate agents and found a listing for a property for sale within forty miles of my mother's last known address. Daddy had always encouraged me to find properties and invest, and I had my own money, but he'd freak out if he learned about my plan. All the same, buying an investment property was something we often discussed. Just not in England. I'd heard it said the best deceptions stuck as close to the truth as possible. If the plan of buying a house in England sounded hair-brained, so be it.

I could always hope I'd never have to tell him specifics, or that I'd taken an excursion across the pond at all.

# Chapter Five

*May 25, WEDNESDAY A.M.*

The jitters didn't disappear once I got on the plane, and my inability to do anything besides sit and wait tortured me. The Strickland deal was set to proceed on June 10th. Until then, the letter writer's threat would hang over my head.

I dug the old Altoids tin out of my pocket, popped it open, and removed the paper lining I'd fashioned so many years ago. A worn, folded drawing fell out.

Like the old key, I'd kept the picture hidden away in the tin, saving it from Daddy's repeated culling of anything reminding him of Mother. She'd sketched a sycamore tree and painted it with cheap watercolors. The blues and greens had faded as much as my memories of her, a thin woman with corn silk hair and deep dimples. She liked to go barefoot, I thought, and her toes were long, but for all I knew, the person I remembered could've been a babysitter. Carefully, I replaced the tiny sketch and tucked it back into its hiding place.

## The Key Collector's Promise

I couldn't believe I'd bought a property on Sycamore Street, sight unseen, chosen over any others simply because of the name.

Antsy, I made a few notes.

*Locate the property on Sycamore Street and settle in. Find a car to rent for the duration. Go to the last place mother resided and scout for information.*

I didn't need such a list, but having it written grounded me. After a while, fatigue caught up, and I nodded off, only to jerk awake every twenty minutes, the dread of an important task undone pressing on my shoulders.

My eyes were wide open when we approached Heathrow. The sky was clear, achingly blue. The wide strip of the Thames snaked its way through brown and smaller patches of green. As rooftops emerged, tiny boats moved about on the surface of the water and, from this view, reminded me of minnows. The plane sliced through a filmy white cloud.

Suspended in a moment of anticipation, I could almost buy into the peaceful lie that in such a beautiful world, all was well. Then, with a rush, gray buildings appeared, erasing my fanciful notion, and dread returned, gnawing at my gut. I reached for the antacids in my purse.

In the awkward shuffle of deboarding, a man bumped me in the aisle. "Sorry, miss."

His gaze flickered over me, and I thought I recognized him. The hair at my nape pricked.

*Don't be ridiculous, Sandra.*

No one was after me. It was my mother they intended to harm. Still, I monitored him long enough to be satisfied that I didn't know him, after all.

Nerves singing, I resented the slowdown forced by the process of collecting luggage and weaving through the crowd. The time difference had bought me six hours. Soon, Addie would unlock the office and listen to the message I'd left on the machine before I'd headed to the airport, a message saying I wasn't coming in to the office today. Small comfort, that tiny space of wiggle room. More explanation would be needed later. If she questioned the timestamp of my late night call, I'd come up with an excuse.

I hailed a cab and went straight to the estate agent's office. The short ride eased my impatience, right up until I arrived. Inside, the office was deserted, save the fortyish secretary, because everyone else had gone to lunch, leaving me waiting in a stiff chair, my Samsonite luggage at my feet.

"Another coffee?" The nervous secretary offered.

"No, thank you. This is fine." Lifting the Styrofoam cup to my lips, I pretended to take a sip. "When will the agent be back?"

"Any time now, I'm sure." She kept eye contact with me and smiled as she fiddled with her wristwatch. "What brings you to our part of the world? Job?" Her eyebrows lifted along with the corners of her mouth.

I had no clue what to say. Me, who could talk a blue streak and redirect as well as any lawyer, rendered incapable. "Yes. My job." Investment property was my job. I took a real sip of the awful coffee.

I felt like a foreigner.

It struck me that I was, and foolish tears pricked my eyes. Would my mother be as uncomfortable in my presence as this lady was?

## The Key Collector's Promise

I lifted my chin. It didn't matter how my mother reacted. I had to warn her.

After I convinced her I wasn't off my rocker.

The agent arrived at five past one o'clock, his suit almost as wrinkled as I felt. He offered to drive me to the property, and I accepted. On the ride, I blamed jet lag for my monosyllabic non-answers.

The Victorian, two-story brick terraced house was painted blue, and twice as tall as it was wide. A low, gray stone wall cut across half the front, where the garden contained a patch of grass, leggy herbs of some kind, and a lone rose bush.

The house trim could use a coat of paint. If I stayed long enough, I'd see to it. If not, surely I could find someone to spruce it up for me to resell.

The agent made to exit the car.

I said, "No need to get out. I can manage, if you'd give me the keys, of course." I was too tired to deal with a showing. At this point, it didn't matter if the roof was about to cave in. I had nowhere else to go.

"Of course," he said. "But let me carry your bags to the door, at least."

I made an effort at politeness. "How kind of you. Thank you."

He kept ahold of the keys, and when he was about to unlock the door of the house, I put out my hand, palm up, and smiled stiffly. If I had to block him, I would.

He shrugged, passed the keys and papers over, then took his leave, motoring off.

Number five was last in the row of terraced houses, and on its other side, a huge, multi-storied brick house sat, looking as if it had been added on to over the years. Somehow, the mixed styles of the dwelling worked.

Natural flora, salty air, and quaint homes reigned. There was even a duck pond. It felt out of time, a place of memory, where threats from my life back in Louisiana couldn't touch me.

Yielding to a strange fancy, I unclasped my necklace, slid the old key from the chain, and tried it in the front door lock. I gasped. It fit. I attempted to give the key a twist, but of course, it didn't turn.

Such foolishness.

My cheeks grew hot. This house didn't look familiar in the least. Had I really supposed I could traipse to England and find the old vacation house, my mother inside waiting for me with lemon curd toast?

I glanced around. Had anyone noticed me? The teen boy riding a bike and two women chatting near a giant sycamore tree in a grassy area appeared oblivious to my foray into fantasy. I stuffed the old key into my purse and used the actual house keys.

Without ceremony, I went inside and turned on the lights, revealing outdated wallpaper, scuffed wood floor, and a battered, skinny table near the entry holding a standard black rotary phone.

Better than I'd hoped for.

I lifted the phone's receiver to my ear. Silent, as expected. No service. I'd been warned of this.

I didn't know a soul here. My fingers found the dips and grooves of the key to the house, tracing the pattern. Without a working phone, who could I turn to if I needed help? A wave of trepidation almost undid me.

## The Key Collector's Promise

Meeting the neighbors as soon as possible seemed a good idea, and I stepped back outside, intending to introduce myself to the two women at the sycamore tree or anyone else around. Not a neighbor greeted my sight, save for a lone woman in the distance, walking away.

A breeze stirred the leaves of the giant sycamore, whispering into the empty street and leaving me twitchy. I ducked back into the house, securely locking the door behind me.

The interior needed an update, but boasted a front room with a fireplace. I went through the small kitchen with its outdated teal cabinets, old white refrigerator, and mismatched dining set, straight to the small conservatory and trailed my fingers over the dusty windows. Beyond the back garden lay the beach, and down the beach stood a lighthouse. The Deben River was a hop, skip, and a jump away, as was the sea. Later, I could put the house up for rent. In a village like this, surely vacation rentals would do well. If—no—*when* Daddy had a conversation with me, I'd tell him I was investing, repairing the home myself, and trying my wings. He wouldn't be happy about the location, but he couldn't fault the idea of an investment rental property.

The old fridge contained not a morsel of food, but I craved only two things, answers and sleep. Answers would have to wait. My body demanded sleep.

I stretched out on the lumpy couch. In the morning, I'd find a phone, make a couple of calls, rent a car, and then begin my search.

## Chapter Six

*May 26, THURSDAY 3:00 A.M. in Eden Cove*

Predictably, I'd wakened at three in the morning and couldn't go back to sleep. I'd resorted to taking a warm shower, but the water turned tepid almost immediately. Not a relaxing experience. I ended up downstairs wedged into a corner of the couch, bundled in my navy cardigan, looking over Mother's file again. I could barely read the pages under the weak light of a wall lamp with gold gimp trim, a sign it was for sixties fashion, not function.

Harlow's notes indicated hospitalizations and possible diabetes, but no confirmation. She'd been employed at a few shops, a pet store, and a candy factory, never staying at any job for long, and there were gaps. A chronic condition could explain the bouncing around and the inability to keep a job, although so could being impulsive and unreliable.

My neck hurt. I stretched and rolled my stiff shoulders. The temperature had dipped, goosebumping my arms. I frowned at the small fireplace. Was it for heat or simply decorative?

I snorted. Like I knew how to build a fire.

## The Key Collector's Promise

Swinging my arms to encourage circulation, I walked over to the windows facing the street. The intermittent light from the lighthouse down the beach and my neighbors' outdoor lights were no match for the blackness. It was even darker in the shadows cast by the large home next door. Outside, two glowing animal eyes appeared, then another pair. Rattled, I stepped back. Dogs? Foxes? The windows had no curtains. I switched the lamp off, creeping myself out even more.

Dark had never bothered me before.

Ghost stories at camp and pranks leaving me locked in a cabin alone overnight had barely gotten a reaction from me. I'd been sure no one would cross my Daddy, and by extension, me.

I wasn't used to being scared, and it made me mad. A strange mad I had nowhere to direct, other than to decide I wouldn't let anything spook me.

I took Mother's file upstairs to the smaller bedroom and sat on the floor, tucked into a corner, away from the window. If I didn't see the animals out there, it shouldn't bother me. But once spooked, I noticed how empty the house was. How alone I was.

I gave myself a mental shake.

Certainly English villages had wildlife, or more likely, house cats out for the night.

I went back to the file. Mother never married, besides Daddy. She had a sister. No parents listed. Were my English grandparents alive? Growing up, I'd yearned for grandparents, and had manufactured grief the way only teenaged girls can. A trace of the sadness remained, and mild curiosity, but I had no time for such musings and refocused on the task at hand.

During the six-year gap since her last known location, Iris could've moved anywhere. Strain as I might, I could not remember her having any unusual habits, hobbies, or notable vices.

I huffed. My inability to produce a single idea beyond my initial plan of asking around at her previous address had me frustrated. An old key and a nondescript watercolor picture of a tree weren't the best of clues, and there wasn't a single thing I could do about the situation until morning.

Antsy, I tackled the practical and roamed the house, noting down items to repair. The conservatory window casings were in sad shape, all the walls could do with stripping and re-papering, and a new hot water heater was a must. Three suspicious stains marked the ceiling on the top floor. One resembled a huge fist, prompting a mental picture of Strickland and his always-present, muscle-bound escorts. The thought chased all list-taking skills away, and my legs turned to jelly. I must warn my mother, but had little to go on, and felt utterly useless.

Religious wasn't a word anyone could apply to me, much less devout, and my church training had been spotty. Stints at Christian school hadn't been due to any faith traditions on Daddy's part, more for the academics and rubbing elbows with the right sort, but I needed God now. Instead of giving in to an impulsive response sparked by a televangelist program, I'd follow the pattern I'd been taught and pray the right way this time.

I bowed my head, hoping God would have pity on me. If not me, then on my mother.

## Chapter Seven

*May 26, THURSDAY Dawn in UK/May 25, WEDNESDAY 10:00 P.M. in US*

A cloud-draped sun peeked over the horizon as I headed for the village shops in search of a phone booth. I'd check in with Harlow first, an easier call than the one to Addie. My stomach knotted at the thought of calling her and the necessary deceptions. How I hated lying to Addie.

Damp chilled me to the bone, and I snugged my cardigan tighter around me, wishing for a jacket. Out of nowhere, a huge black cat darted across my path, and I clapped my hands over my mouth, capturing a shriek. The cat ran ahead, turned, and twitched his ears.

Crazy cat.

No doubt he'd been one of the creatures watching me from the neighborhood bushes the night before, scaring me. I let out a strangled laugh. Aerobics not required for an elevated heart rate this morning.

A misty drizzle wet my hair, hurrying me toward the shops. The rain paused long enough for me to catch the end of a full sunrise over the North Sea. Light glinted off the surface of the water, setting the stage for a postcard-perfect moment. If only I were here on my long-wished-for vacation and reunion, rather than a rushed, anxiety-ridden trip. A blink later, clouds obscured the sight.

I should've enjoyed it while it lasted.

A red, modern telephone booth—easy to spot—came into view and beyond it, the post office. I hurried to the phone, ducked inside, and wiggled my MCI long-distance card out of my back pocket.

I dialed Harlow. His machine clicked on. I opened my mouth to speak, but he picked up before I had the chance.

"What is it? I charge extra after hours."

I ignored his grousing. Sure, it was late, but barely ten o'clock back home.

I said, "It's Sandra. Have you got any updates?"

His sigh filled the line. "I wish, but no. Listen, let me know how you're doing over there."

"Sure." Disappointment clogged my throat. So much for last-minute miracle clues from Harlow.

"What's the number where you're staying?"

"I'm calling from a phone box."

"Near the hotel?"

His fishing for information sent my antennae up. As a free agent, Harlow owed loyalty to no one. He didn't know my address, but I'd mentioned Eden Cove, hadn't I? Maybe. Probably. I had to stop trusting people.

"Need to go, Harlow. I'll be in touch soon." I hung up the receiver and jerked back as if the hard plastic burned.

## The Key Collector's Promise

The panic hitching a ride on my back made it easier to call Addie. She'd be home, winding down and finishing her favorite show, *Dynasty*.

Addie fussed at me for going AWOL, but calmed quicker than I expected, especially once I'd given the excuse of finding an investment property and deciding to take a chance on it. I didn't mention England. She tut-tutted, and I let her, but extracted a promise.

"I want to make a go of this project on my own. Don't tell Daddy until I can talk to him, Addie." I ran my fingernails along the tiny ledge beneath the phone. "Promise me."

In the end, she did, which might buy me a few days, at most.

I paged through the phonebook in search of a car rental agency. A flash of color whizzed past, and in my periphery, I caught sight of a lanky young guy on a bicycle, the teenage boy I'd seen the day before on Sycamore Street. I stepped out of the phone box and watched him disappear behind an older stone structure with a tile roof, Ferryman's Bakery, according to the sign.

A definite scent of fresh bread floated in the air, and my stomach rumbled. Perhaps someone at the bakery would know of a local place to rent a car, and at the same time, I could get a bite to eat. I neared the building, muted conversation and laughter drawing me forward. The rain had tapered off some, but my soaked, blue Adidas Starsky shoes squished with each step.

Along the front of the bakery, purple irises grew. Iris, like my mother's name. The familiar blooms cheered me, until I read the closed sign,

What I wouldn't do for a cup of coffee and a piece of whatever smelled so good.

I slogged back the way I'd come and was halfway down the path when a woman's voice behind me said, "Hello? Are you lost?"

*Lost?*

It was a good word to describe me at the moment.

Doing an about-face, I found a middle-aged woman wearing an apron and a friendly smile.

I smiled back into her periwinkle-blue eyes and said, "I've bought a place in Eden Cove and got in late last night. There's not a speck of food in the house. I was using the public phone and smelled the bread baking. Decided to follow my nose, not realizing you weren't open yet."

"Oh!" She wiped her hands on her apron. "You're the new neighbor! In number five?"

I blinked. "Yes."

So people had noticed me. Of course, they would in such a small, tightly packed space.

"Well, we can't have a new neighbor wandering about hungry." She glanced at the sky. "And in the rain, to boot. Come on in." Waving me forward, she disappeared into the bakery.

The woman moved fast, and I hustled to keep up.

Over her shoulder, she said, "We live on Sycamore." She inhaled and hollered, "Kenny!" Without pause, she indicated a small table and two chairs. "Sit down. Our specialty is Italian coffee and pastry, along with our famous scones, but we also have fresh sweet rolls, if you prefer. Kenny can bring you tea, juice, or milk."

## The Key Collector's Promise

A man yelled at someone in the back, and a younger male voice returned with a protest. A clatter of pans followed.

My cheeks flushed. I'd clearly intruded. "I know it's early, and I don't want to bother. Whatever is handy is fine. I'm not picky." In case my offhand comment offended, I quickly amended. "It all sounds wonderful."

"Don't you let those two back there scare you off." Despite the worry creases on her forehead, she smiled a what-can-you-do smile and shrugged. "Growing pains. Hard on parents and teenagers, both."

I nodded, not that I knew anything about raising teens.

As if suddenly becoming aware she'd been too revealing, she blushed and cleared her throat. "Well, at least we have excellent scones." She pointed to a sign on the wall. "Says so right there." She winked, an attempt to lighten the mood.

I chuckled, and it seemed to please her. She was such a lovely woman. The male conversation in back changed tone to apologetic, and she nodded to herself and hurried away, trailing worry.

Her family was lucky to have her.

She hadn't told me her first name, but I'd already decided I'd be buying my bread and cakes at Ferryman's for the duration of my stay. I liked Mrs. Ferryman. Then I remembered I was in Eden Cove on a mission, not vacation, and all the warm fuzzies evaporated.

A red-faced teen, Kenny, I presumed, approached with a plate containing four huge buns. He flipped his sandy, shoulder-length hair out of his hazel eyes and set the food in front of me.

"What to drink?"

"Coffee." The response was automatic. I added, "If there's any already brewed."

"We have coffee. Be right back."

I picked up a bun and set to feeding my belly. It was the second day in a row I'd had a bakery treat. I put the bun down. I could almost hear Conner mocking me.

A short time after we'd stopped dating, he'd brought me a glazed donut on a napkin. He'd said, "You look like you could use this." Then he'd shot me a quirky grin.

Mocking.

As if he hadn't noticed me picking at celery and rice cakes at my desk all week. Maybe it had been part of the competition between us.

He'd never said why he'd lost interest in dating. True, he'd been coolly upset about me winning a client he'd worked hard to build a rapport with before I'd swooped in and charmed the client. But he'd done the same to me, snatching away a possible sale from one of my high school classmates simply because I'd been out of the office. Daddy encouraged friendly competition.

Reflecting on our past interactions had me reassessing. I'd assumed his office behavior was spurred by business rivalry and the inability to take as good as he got. What if he had a darker motive? Conner Harrison could be the mysterious letter writer.

I sighed. As could half of Bienville Parish.

It was too much to puzzle out before breakfast and coffee. I went back to my bun. Forget the calories. Besides, I'd eaten next to nothing in the last forty-eight hours.

Kenny returned with two Styrofoam cups of coffee, gave me one, and took a seat opposite. "Mum said you're new on our street, yeah?"

Covering my mouth, I swallowed a piece of bun and nodded. I sipped the coffee. "Just moved in."

"Yeah." He did the hair flip again. "I saw someone was there. Welcome to the neighborhood."

"Thank you for welcoming me."

The tips of his ears pinked, and he squirmed a little.

I said, "Do you know the closest place I can rent a car?"

"Rick has a car." The boy slurped his coffee and eyed the remaining buns.

Rick? A friend most likely. I wasn't eager to have a discussion about a teenage boy's car.

I scooted the plate closer to him. "Take one."

He darted a gaze toward the back of the bakery. "I shouldn't."

"It's fine. I offered."

With another stealthy glance behind him, he reached for a bun. He took huge bites, chewing furiously. Afraid to ask another question until he got the thing down, I waited and tried to remember how to perform the Heimlich maneuver in case he started choking to death.

As soon as he finished, I repeated, "I need to rent a car. Do you know the closest place?"

He looked at me as if I were dense. "The mechanic garage. Rick has a car."

"I see. That's perfect."

Not exactly Hertz. I didn't know how perfect it would be, but I'd check it out.

The front door eased open. A slim woman with a fluff of cropped blonde hair stuck her head in and met my gaze. Her blue eyes widened. "Oh. Hello." She slipped through the door. Another clatter of pans came from the back of the bakery, but the young woman acted as if she didn't hear it and extended her hand. "I'm Harriet. I see you've met my brother, Kenny."

There must've been a ten-year gap between the siblings.

"I'm Sandra."

We shook, and she withdrew her hand, turning to Kenny. "I've got to run Jennifer to the doctor's. She has a temperature." Frowning, she squinted at the remnants of my breakfast in front of her brother. Hands on hips, she said, "Kenny, what are you doing?"

He straightened as if goosed, shaking his head in immediate denial of his sister's insinuation. "Nothing. Mum told me to welcome her to the neighborhood."

"There's crumbs on your chin, and only one plate here. A plate that's in front of you, not our new neighbor."

Kenny scooted his chair back and stood. "Gotta go."

I hastened to explain to Harriet. "It's all right. I practically forced him to eat one."

"I'm sure you had to twist his arm." More amused than annoyed, she rolled her eyes. "Boys. He's good at heart. Listen, I've got to run, but please do come pop by number three if you need help navigating the neighborhood or anything. My husband and I live on Sycamore Street, too. Mum and Dad are in number one." An amused smile parted her pink lips, revealing small, straight teeth, and she suddenly appeared younger. "But you've already found where to buy the best sticky buns in Suffolk. That's a good start."

I couldn't help but return her grin.

# Chapter Eight

*May 26, THURSDAY Midmorning*

As it turned out, Rick was more talkative than Kenny. By the time I'd procured the use of an older beige Renault adorned with a few rust spots, the friendly mechanic had regaled me with all sorts of driving advice in addition to warning me about strangers and unscrupulous business owners, none of whom lived in his village of Eden Cove.

"Now, there may be a few rambunctious boys about." He pushed back his worn cap and scratched his clean-shaven jaw. "I've had to chase them off for messing about with the rubbish bins."

"Gangs?"

"Oh, no. Just kids being kids. A couple of them from the next village over made a sort of clubhouse in number five last summer, sneaking in at night, what with it being empty so often. There was a huge stink over it when the owners found out. I suppose that's why they finally sold it."

Great. No telling what hidden damage the house had. I made a mental note to do another check of the house.

When Rick asked me about my family, I got the prickles. I hated to mislead but found myself assuring him my family would soon be with me, which was true, in a way. Either I would find my mother, or Daddy would find me.

I gave Rick a wave as I took my leave.

The sun broke up the clouds, tinting the gray skies blue in the promise of a clear day and, eager to head to my mother's last known address, I had to force myself to return to the terraced house for dry shoes.

When I reached the end of Sycamore Street, an older lady came out of number four, still a distance away. The silver-haired, trim-figured woman carried a walking stick, but going by her steady, purposeful stride, certainly didn't seem to need it. As we drew nearer each other, I nodded and smiled, and she returned the gesture. It would be wise to know who belonged in the neighborhood and who didn't. I slowed my pace. If the woman wanted a chat, I hoped she was less verbose than Rick or I'd never get on with my mission. The woman passed me by, as intent on going her way as I was on mine. At least I knew my neighbor's face now.

Once inside my front door, I toed off my shoes. My wet footprints followed me as I walked to my half-unpacked suitcase and dug out brown loafers.

I'd need Wellies.

A memory of yellow boots and being called ducky sprang to mind, and with it came tears. Where had that come from? I wiped my eyes and yanked on the boots. I had no time for tears or memories.

## The Key Collector's Promise

Mother's previous address was in a run-down housing complex of flats. In the manager's office, the front area had a couple of worn upholstered orange chairs, a full ashtray stand wedged between them, and behind a desk, a plump, middle-aged woman with a phone receiver pressed to her ear.

The woman swiveled away, pretending she hadn't noticed me.

I coughed. Then coughed again.

Feigning surprise, she blinked her frosted eyelids and muttered into the phone, "I'll call you back."

She poked a pen into her mass of auburn helmet hair. "Help you?" Besides dripping annoyance, her voice sounded uncannily like a honk, and it chased my confidence right out the door like so many startled pigeons.

I wasn't one to shrink back, but I was a stranger in a strange land, unable to get my footing.

The woman stood and picked up a clipboard, a clear signal she had things to do.

Lack of confidence aside, I carried on. "I'm looking for the manager?"

"That's me," she said.

Behind me, the door opened, and I jumped. A burly guy in blue coveralls came in. He touched his cap and nodded at me. A handyman. An expected person to be at an apartment complex. I nodded back, trying to control my twanging nerves and act normal.

Cloak and dagger wasn't my forte.

I turned to the manager, meeting her bored stare.

Off-balance, I fumbled for words. "Hi. Hate to interrupt, but I'm looking for my…mum. She used to live here, and I came from the States. I'm trying to locate her."

This perked her up, and she asked for my mother's name and when she'd been a resident. Aware of the man behind me, I explained who I was looking for, but not the why.

With a shake of her head, she said, "Sorry, love. Never heard of her. I've only been here for eighteen months. Why did you need to find her? Win the lotto?" She laughed at her own joke.

"No. Just want to find her."

"Ah, well. I can't tell what I don't know." Her interest had faded as soon as the prospect of a juicy story had disappeared.

If she only knew.

She looked past me. "Hey, Charlie. There's a bit of trouble with the pipes in fourteen. I'll take you up."

I couldn't give in. "Could I get the previous manager's contact information?"

Grimacing, she scratched her hair, and the whole mass shifted as one entity. "I can't do that." Any sympathy had leaked away.

"The owner? Surely I can talk to the owner."

"I'm not sure."

"What about other employees? Or older residents?"

With a jangle of keys, the man stepped up beside me, and I opened my mouth to protest his interruption. This was my best lead.

He said, "Come on, Millie. Have a heart. Just give her the information. She's looking for her mum."

Millie the Manager grumbled and sat down at her desk. She flipped open an address book, scribbled on a scrap of paper, and handed it to me. "That's the owner, but don't call before ten or after five." She frowned. "Don't tell him you got the number from me. I must be crazy to stick my neck out."

## The Key Collector's Promise

The guy in coveralls grinned. "I knew you were an old softie, Millie."

She grunted but then batted her eyelashes at the guy.

He nodded at me. "Best of luck to you."

My thanks were lost as the two started discussing plumbing problems.

The manager hadn't said I couldn't knock on doors, so I didn't leave the complex right away. Instead, I started at the unit farthest from the office, working my way around until I found a person who remembered my mother.

The elderly lady used a walker, and her head bobbled on her thin neck. "Iris had diabetes, right?"

My pulse sped up. "That's right."

Harlow hadn't found irrefutable facts on my mother's health history but had noted diabetes as a possibility.

"Poor dear." The elderly woman tut-tutted.

I almost stopped breathing. Was this lady about to tell me my mother had died?

She said, "If I remember correctly, she had to go to a care home."

"What was the name of the facility?"

"I couldn't say. We weren't really friends other than to nod in passing. I haven't heard anything about Iris for quite some time, but I'm positive she went to a care home."

# Chapter Nine

*May 26, THURSDAY Afternoon*

I knocked on every door in the apartment complex, but at least half the residents weren't home, or didn't answer, and the rest didn't know Iris. The care home idea was the only lead I unearthed. I tried not to bank on the information. The woman, named June, had been eager to please, and elderly. At one point, she'd called me Janice, never noticing her mistake, and asked me to tea, which I'd politely declined.

I wasn't sure her information was reliable. Still, a lead was a lead.

Workers at the closest shops didn't remember Iris. I canvassed the area until a blue-uniformed bobby started shadowing me. A police encounter wasn't on my agenda, and I decided to go back to Eden Cove, let my fingers do the walking from the house. By now the phone should be connected. I stopped by a post office and riffled through the telephone directory provided for the public, jotting down numbers. The temptation to tear a page out almost won over, but the memory of the police officer I'd spotted earlier squelched the desire.

## The Key Collector's Promise

On the drive back to Eden Cove, I cranked up the radio, a feeble attempt to drown out my parade of worries. It was only afternoon, but the day had already been ridiculously long, and at the sight of thatched roofs and slate roofs, stone and brick walls of the village houses, my spirit lifted. A quick stop to get groceries, return to number five, make a few phone calls, and locate the care home. It sounded like a doable plan.

I bought oranges, a packet of chicken, and coffee, plus a few other necessities, loaded them into the Renault, and settled behind the wheel. I was feeling pretty good, all things considered.

Until I tried to start the car.

The ignition made a grinding noise, and I pumped furiously on the gas, muttering under my breath, "Don't do this to me, car."

The engine caught, died, and whined before fading to complete silence.

Dead.

I rested my forehead on the steering wheel. My feet hurt, my eyes were gritty, and I wanted to wash up and eat before life piled on another problem. Was that too much to ask? I smacked the dash of the old car, got out, and retrieved my sack of groceries.

Rick's was in my line of sight, and I could easily go by, but thirty minutes of chit-chat? No. I'd walk to the house on Sycamore Street and call him from there. He could retrieve the car from the grocer's.

On the way to the house, I peeled an orange, ate it, and felt better—from the fresh air or the food, I didn't know. Both, probably.

The phone numbers I'd collected demanded attention, and the minute I got inside number five, I propped my bag of groceries on one hip and lifted the handset of the old rotary phone to my ear. A dial tone greeted me. Connected. Thank goodness. My first call was to Rick, who told me he'd take care of the car "straight away" and have it back in business. After I got off the call, I stowed the perishable groceries in the fridge, grabbed a soda, and headed back to the phone.

I dialed the number Millie the Manager had provided. The previous apartment manager had passed away, and his widow didn't know a thing about my mother or any possible contacts.

I dragged the phone off the old entryway table, sat cross-legged on the floor, and started dialing, beginning with the first care home on my list. Strike one. I continued through the rest, and got to the end with no luck.

Now what?

Maybe the elderly lady from the apartments had been mistaken, or maybe I hadn't cast my net wide enough.

I paced from the kitchen to the front door and back again. With no car, options were limited. If only I'd written more phone numbers, I could keep calling around. Maybe Harriet, the young mother from number three, had a directory. Hadn't she said to pop by if I needed anything? My Starskys were damp, but I put them on anyway.

I opened the door, startled to find a medium-sized, shaggy brown dog sitting on my front step. I wasn't afraid of dogs, but he'd spooked me, appearing out of nowhere. He cocked his head sideways as if asking what the trouble was. I realized I'd been clutching my chest and let go of my shirt, smoothing the fabric.

Frowning, I said, "You can't blame me for being surprised." I leaned out the doorway and craned my neck side to side. Not a soul in sight. "Where do you belong, pup?"

The dog barked, ran to the street and back again, stopping to give me an expectant look. I grabbed my light jacket and stepped outside. No longer in an all-fired hurry, the dog sniffed around my pink rose bush, lifted a leg, and watered the plant.

"Really, dog?"

The rose bush was the only bright spot in the front. I shook my head. Like it mattered.

The dog darted to number three, Harriet's home, and took up sentry at the end of the walkway.

"So you belong here?" I squinted at the next home on the row of terraced houses, a replica of my own, except for bricks a different color, a different door, and no rose bush. Weird how the dog led me to my intended destination. At my knock, Harriet opened the door, her fluffy hair haloing her tired face. A greenish splotch stained her light pink blouse.

"Oh, hi," she said.

I gestured to the dog. "Yours?"

She tucked her chin into her neck. "Noooo. I have enough on my hands without adding a pet."

"Sorry. He stopped right at your place. I was coming by to see if you had a phone directory."

"A phone directory? I don't think so." A child's wail erupted from the recesses of the house, and Harriet looked over her shoulder. "I'll ask Mum if she has one."

"How's your little girl? Jennifer, right? I remember you said you were taking her to the doctor. I hope she's all right."

Harriet's face opened like a flower budding in spring daylight, and I got a peek at the pretty young woman beneath

45

the worried mum. "Thanks. She'll be fine. Just a cold." She paused. "I'd ask you in, but the place is a wreck, what with my two-year-old being sick."

"Oh, no," I said, flustered. Had she thought I was angling for an invitation? "I just wondered about the phone directory. And the dog." Lamely, I gestured to the pup like a game show beauty, embarrassing myself further.

"If I hear of anyone missing a dog, I'll send them around."

We said our goodbyes.

At the street, I hesitated. There'd been a directory in the phone box. And I could check at the post office. That's what I'd do.

Right on cue, the sky spluttered, and the rain picked up. I decided a little rain never hurt anyone. The dog seemed to agree, keeping pace with me.

It seemed I'd picked up a furry companion, at least for a while.

## Chapter Ten

*May 26, THURSDAY Late Afternoon*

The walk to the post office soaked me, but the dog kept pace, never so much as pausing at another house.

I ran the last few steps to the phone box and ducked inside. Where the phone book should be, an empty cord dangled. Handiwork of the prank-pulling kids Rick had warned me about? Grumbling under my breath, I made for the post office, splashing through puddles and soaking my jeans up to my ankles. I tugged the handle. The door didn't budge.

Closed.

I leaned forward and bumped my head on the glass.

Rain dripped down my neck.

With a sigh, I told the dog, "Come on."

All the way back, the dog kept growling at the rain, making me jumpy. I picked up the pace, more than once peering behind me into the downpour, seeing nothing out of the ordinary. When the blue bricks of number five came into view, I breathed easier.

The dog bolted after a small animal, a cat or maybe a rabbit. No telling what was in the surrounding bushes. Hesitating at my front door, I waited a minute for him, but he was busy, and I was wet. If he wanted in, he knew how to bark.

I unlocked my door, and a musty odor brought on by the damp pinched my nose. The sad barrenness of the interior, made extra gloomy by the overcast sky and late hour despite all the windows, was a perfect illustration of my failure.

I'd been so sure I could find Iris.

Flopping onto the lumpy old couch, I covered my face. If Addie were here, she'd tell me tomorrow would be better. If Daddy were here, he'd tell me to buck up.

Neither admonition helped.

I toed off my shoes and peeled off my socks. Blue dye from my shoes had stained the white cotton, so I carried the socks to the bathroom sink and flung them in. I scrubbed at the spots, but it did no good.

Where was a laundromat around here?

A hysterical giggle escaped me. I was in a foreign country, with no car and no contacts. Evil men were after my mother, and I didn't have a clue how to find her.

Why on earth was I worried about blue-stained socks?

I stared at myself in the mirror. Circles ringed my eyes, and my bloodless lips were set in a grim line. Tears came, and I ground the heels of my palms into my eye sockets.

How I hated crying.

I'd passed my physical limit and needed sleep. That was all. I'd been going non-stop since I'd opened the terrible note.

A sharp rap at my front door sent my pulse rocketing. I was as jumpy as a deer during hunting season. I unrolled a strip of toilet paper and blew my nose, then dabbed my face with a damp cloth.

It would do. I went to the door.

Across the threshold, a wide-eyed Harriet stood holding a plastic grocery bag. "I, er…found a directory. Are you all right?"

"Yes." I bit my lip. Maybe in this situation, a smidge of honesty was best. "No. I mean, come in. It's raining buckets."

It wasn't anymore, but she didn't correct me.

"I don't want to barge in."

My nose ran and more tears welled up. I dug the tissue out of my pocket and dabbed them away.

"Oh, dear." She entered and placed the directory beside the phone on the little table. Her pretty, worried mom-face scrunched up. "Are you in trouble?"

Her kindness did me in. The next thing I knew, I started blabbing.

"I need to find my mother. My birth mother." I clarified. I stepped over to the couch and plopped down.

Harriet perched next to me. "And you're upset about it?"

I took a breath.

How to explain without sounding melodramatic?

"Well," I picked my words carefully. "I *do* need to locate my mother. I've always wanted to, but I'm also trying to go about it quietly. There's a man. I'd rather he didn't know where I was."

Harriet's face grew rigid with alarm. "A man? Here?"

Immediately, I shook my head to reassure her. "No, no. In America."

"But you think he might trace you? A fellow who won't take no for an answer, I'd guess."

"Yes. That's it exactly."

"Are you quite well? I mean, do you need to see a doctor, or the police?" She inhaled and paused. "St. Bartholomew's offers help and counseling for battered women."

I said, "Oh, no. It's fine. I don't need a doctor or anything like that."

So, I hadn't *exactly* given her the right idea. I was concerned Strickland's goons would hurt my mother, not running from an ex, but her assumption hit close enough to the truth. Didn't it? Besides, it was better she didn't know the details.

She patted my knee. "I'd guess having an ocean between you should help. Of course, all of us in the neighborhood will be on alert for any strange people lurking about." She sat back and looked around. "Now, then. I'll go put your kettle on."

"Oh. I don't have one."

Her lips puckered. Her brows knit. She blinked a few times, seeming more affronted by the fact that I didn't have a kettle than about any danger from the mysterious person I alluded to.

I hastened to say, "I can get one tomorrow." If I felt the need.

"How can a person face a regular day, much less trauma of this sort with not a crumb of food or single tea bag in the house?" Flushing, Harriet paused and rearranged her face to a calm expression. She cleared her throat. "Is the dog still around?"

"He ran off."

"Maybe he went home."

She continued talking about dogs, pets, and children for a few minutes. "In any event, I've brought you the directory. You'll be all right?"

"Yes. I will." I pushed my hair from my face. "I just let things get to me."

## The Key Collector's Promise

Feather-light, she touched my shoulder. "We all do, at times." Flipping to the front page of the directory, she pointed to an inked list. "Here's Mum and Dad, The Ferrymans. They live in number one. And right next door to you, in number four, is Amy. She's older, but a good person to have looking out for you. Retired SOE, but still sharp as a tack." Harriet raised her eyebrows as if I should know what the acronym meant.

I nodded, making a mental note to find out. I remembered my neighbor, the walker. "Are you sure Amy is okay with me having her number?"

"Of course." Harriet waved a hand. "I've known her forever, and she's a wonderful lady. Look, I'll put my number right here at the top, if you bring me a pen."

Harriet was a sweet young woman. In another life, we could've been friends.

I dug a Lejeune's Realty promo pen out of my purse and almost told her to keep it, but caught myself in time. She might leave it somewhere. Caution was the name of the game if I meant to stay a step ahead of Strickland, or Daddy. It felt like overkill, but leaving a trail of clues about my location wasn't smart.

# Chapter Eleven

*May 26, THURSDAY Evening*

After Harriet left, I used the directory to look up care homes I'd missed the first time around. After five calls in a row with disinterested personnel or no answer at all, I realized I needed to think up a better plan, but my head pounded, short-circuiting my problem solving skills. I retrieved a small bottle of over-the-counter painkiller from my purse, and fumbled with the tamper resistant packaging, a terrible reminder of the dangers around every corner in today's world. They'd never caught whoever had been responsible for the Tylenol tragedy, poisoning innocent victims. Even medicine wasn't safe from evil people. What chance did I have against nefarious characters intent on harm?

The thought made me nauseous.

In the kitchen, I got a glass of water and swallowed the pills. I'd just placed the empty glass in the sink when I heard something right outside. A child's cry? I froze, holding my breath, straining to listen.

There, it came again.

## The Key Collector's Promise

Beyond the kitchen window, the back garden and the landscape revealed nothing amiss. I crept into the conservatory and stared out of the windows. Nothing was out there. It was my imagination. The warning flashes of the lighthouse down the beach did my headache no favors, and I decided I was being silly.

Then a faint scratching sent chill bumps racing up my spine. I cocked my head, listening. Silence. Nothing but a branch from the tree near the house rubbing against a window, I told myself. The wind.

The cry came again.

Heart in my throat, I cracked the conservatory door. Near the bottom of the opening, a doggie snout appeared and retreated, followed by a whine. The dog. I laughed, a shaky sound, nearly as pitiful as the dog's whine.

With an exaggerated sigh, I opened the door wider. "Come on, then."

He bounded in, tail whirling like a propeller, and performed a full-body shake. I'd never been so glad to receive a doggy-shower. At least if anyone intruded, he could bark a warning.

Besides, he needed me.

I cooked chicken in the old black stove, and a garlicky scent filled the house, setting my mouth watering. I'd subsisted on vending machine snacks and soda with nothing healthy in my system for days, save the one orange.

No wonder I'd been a headachey, emotional wreck.

The dog sat at my feet.

"You wouldn't be foolish enough to pass up a chicken dinner for a vending machine snack, would you?"

His tail thumped against the linoleum floor. He nuzzled my leg and made a noise sounding more human than dog, part whine, part friendly growl, and I scratched him behind the ears.

When the food was ready, I chopped up chicken and mixed it with shredded bread for the dog. I put it in a chipped yellow bowl and planted it in front of him. "Don't get too comfortable. I'm putting out found dog notices tomorrow."

He ignored me and wolfed down the food.

The dog settled the house, gave it a homey feel. The tension in my neck receded, and I stretched out on the couch. My headache had nearly vanished, and I was bone weary, but sleep remained a stranger. I hadn't called Daddy yet. The only thing worse than calling him would be not calling. I couldn't risk him tracking me down and showing up on my doorstep. For three days, anxiety, suspicions, and half-formed plans for finding my mother had endlessly chased each other around in my mind like wind-up bunnies on a mechanical racetrack. I was exhausted.

The dog wriggled in beside me until his head rested on my thigh. He'd need a bath tomorrow. I stroked his fur and listened to his snuffling doggy sighs until sleep finally claimed me.

Next morning, I fed the dog leftover chicken and peeled myself an orange. Rick's Garage wouldn't open for another hour.

The dog's nails clicked on the old linoleum as he came over and leaned against my leg.

"Needy, aren't we?" I didn't know if I referred to him or me.

In short order, I took care of morning necessities, bathed, and dressed in a pullover and pleated twill pants. Put my hair in a ponytail. Found dry shoes. Everywhere I went, the dog followed.

Trust me to acquire a guardian angel with chicken breath and smelly fur.

My finger was in the rotary dial of the phone, about to call Rick's when Harriet showed up, a pink bandana covering her hair.

She shoved a large cardboard box at me. "Here."

"What?"

An assortment of pans, linens, and—yes—a kettle, were piled in the box.

"I can't take this!" My face grew hot. Did she think I had no resources? "I planned to go shopping soon." I hadn't. It wasn't a priority.

"Now you won't have to. At least not for these things." Smug as anything, she said, "You may as well take them. They were headed for the jumble sale." She dusted her hands off. "Must run." Without a backward glance, she did a finger wave over her shoulder.

The dog gave a happy yip.

Ganged up on, that's what it was. Ganged up on by a fairy godmother in a pink kerchief and a fuzzy guardian angel. A smile tugged at the corner of my lips. The first real one since…

The thought of the letter wiped the grin right off my face.

After I picked up the car, and all the way to the city, I worried if the dog had enough food and water or if he'd gotten out of the back garden. Ridiculous. He'd been fine without me before. He'd be fine now. Besides, he wasn't my dog. I felt a twinge of guilt for not posting more than two found dog notices, but I hadn't had time. Everyone stopped at Ferryman's Bakery anyway, and I'd put one there. They'd see the notice if they were looking.

I wheeled into the complex of flats and parked as far away from the manager's office as I could. One encounter with Millie was enough, though I planned on visiting June, the older lady I'd met at the apartments previously and brought a tote with a couple of oranges and some goodies from Ferryman's Bakery for her. I'd see her last, and left the fruit and bread in the car for the time being.

This time around, I found a different set of people, but the same set of answers. No one remembered Iris.

I retrieved the tote and trudged to June's door. When she saw me, her face lit up, and that cheered me a little.

She said, "It's you!"

I offered the tote. "Hello, June. I brought you bread and jam, and a little fruit."

"How lovely! Come in." She took the bag from me and wobbled alarmingly in her walker.

Afraid she'd fall over, I reached for the tote. "Let me get that."

Taking a few steps into the cluttered flat, I put the groceries on the first cleared surface I saw, a small octagon-shaped table beside a worn gold damask armchair that had seen better days.

She beamed at me. "Stay for tea?"

"I'm sorry, not today." I winced, feeling bad for refusing a second time, but I was on a mission. "Just came by to see if you'd remembered anything else. Maybe the name of the care home Iris went to?"

## The Key Collector's Promise

She placed her index finger to the side of her nose. "You know, I've been thinking about it."

My mouth went dry.

"It's on the tip of my tongue, but I can't quite recall. All I can seem to remember is something like summer. Summerdale, maybe?" She frowned. "But that's not right. I'm sorry." Scowling, she tapped her forehead with one knuckle.

"Well, it's something. It's very helpful, and I appreciate it."

It gave me a place to start, at least.

I said, "Did Iris have any regular visitors or friends I might ask?"

"None I can recall." Her quivery fingers plucked at the bag of bread and oranges. "Maybe I'll remember later. You could come back." She sounded wistful.

The apartment must be a lonely place.

I blew out a breath. "I'll leave you my number. You can call if you remember anything."

It was doubtful she knew any more than she had told me on the first visit, but maybe she would remember more. And now I had a name.

Summerdale.

# Chapter Twelve

*May 29, SUNDAY*

The weekend hadn't brought me any closer to finding my mother. The last place I visited had been a variation on summer. Somerset. There was no care home called Summerdale that I could locate, but June had said she only *thought* it was something like summer. She hadn't been sure at all. Perhaps it was all a wild goose chase.

The smell of disinfectant and floral air freshener clung to me. During my visits to care homes, Sunday lunchtime had come and gone.

What was I doing parked in the lot at St. Bartholomew? Looking for answers?

I took in the ancient stone walls of the church and the stained glass windows. For generations, people had worshipped and sought answers within the sanctuary of St. Bartholomew's.

At the last care home, a facility outside London, I'd run out of steam.

The visiting area had been clean and bright, with potted plants and an oversized picture window letting in sunshine, and the people all sang hymns. The residents had been happy to see family members.

An elderly woman in a lavender floral top, her white hair curled, coral lipstick painting her thin mouth, sat in a wheelchair close to the entrance, watching, waiting. I hadn't been able to tear myself away as hope leaked from her, souring into petulance.

I'd understood her far better than the cheerful, stalwart souls singing hymns in the visiting room.

Now, St. Bart's in front of me, I gazed at the old church. I believed in God. Why couldn't I dredge up the joy others could? My situation wasn't any harder than what the people in the care home faced, certainly. Everyone had their trials.

A man came out of the church, the vicar? I reacted as if I'd been caught trespassing and started the car, pretending I hadn't seen him.

At number five, I immediately let in the dog. He jumped up and I buried my face in his fur. Whining, he nosed my chin.

"Never mind me, pup." I sighed. "Just a bad day."

He seemed unsure and stayed close to my side, even after I put food down for him, until I began stuffing myself with pasta.

Taking as long as was possible, I cleaned up the kitchen, washing the few dishes and wiping the counters. I brewed a cup of tea and let it go cold.

Unable to prolong it any longer, I called Daddy.

"Addie told me what you're up to."

Cold sweat broke out all over my body. "What?"

His sigh came through the line loud and clear, not losing an ounce of exasperation by traveling across the ocean. "No need to be so melodramatic about your project. Just make a reasonable profit. That's all I ask."

The property. The story I'd told Addie. My bid to prove myself.

I lifted my chin. "Count on it."

The sad state of the front room mocked me, and I grimaced. This place was more of a drain than a money-maker.

"You'll make something of it, I have no doubt," he replied, dryly.

No disapproval? No rant?

After picking my jaw up from the floor, I changed the topic in case he started breathing fire, reminding him to ask Addie to pick up his suits from the cleaner, to write a donation check for the community renewal fund, and to prepare for his upcoming interview with the local paper.

"I know, I know." He sighed into the phone again, but this time I could tell he wasn't annoyed.

Touched? Pleased? As usual, I didn't know for sure. Daddy was a mystery.

"Be good," he commanded and disconnected the call.

Slowly, I replaced the handset in the cradle.

It had been too easy. Daddy was as sharp as they came. Why hadn't he wanted more details?

He hadn't even asked where I was.

## Chapter Thirteen

*May 30 MONDAY Morning*

During our heart-to-heart, I'd told Harriet about my plans to fix up the place. She'd suggested Kenny as hired help, likely to watch over me. I knew my odd, cautious behavior and my disclosures about Iris, not to mention a bad guy after me, had stirred her concern.

The call with Daddy had set a fire under me to start renovations, proof of my reason for being in Eden Cove. There were plenty of tasks Kenny could help with, and while he worked, I'd regroup. I'd devised a plan to do an expanded search for Iris by plotting out target places on a map, then locating numbers in the Yellow Pages. I could make my calls while Kenny worked.

As soon as I thought it wasn't too early, I phoned Harriet.

"I'll tell him to be there at ten o'clock," she said above the wails of Jennifer's demands for a bunny, or that's what it sounded like. "Does that suit?"

"Sounds great."

We hung up.

Ten o'clock gave me time to pick up the supplies we'd need. At one shop, I found peach paint at a bargain price and stocked up. It would work for almost any room, and I had the car to carry it home in. When I was nearly done with my purchases, I remembered Harriet saying it boggled the mind a human could eat such quantities as a teenage boy, yet remain gangly and thin. Buying snacks was a good excuse to stop into Ferryman's Bakery. I bought buns, which I knew Kenny would be pleased with, and asked Mrs. Ferryman what else he liked. As his mother, she'd know best.

"Goodness. No need to feed him." She pursed her lips. "Just send him on home to eat."

"But I want to get him something. I insist." I crossed my arms.

Mrs. Ferryman knew stubborn when she saw it. "All right. Get him a shepherd's pie, and he'll be happy."

Really? Sounded healthier than pizza, my idea of what teens liked to eat, and I wasn't about to argue with her.

I bobbed my head. "Shepherd's pie it is."

"I'm happy you're giving number five some attention. We'll all be glad to have a young person like yourself living in the village."

I didn't correct the assumption I'd be staying. "It's a nice place." Forcing a smile, I lifted my bag of buns. "Must go. They'll be at the house before I know it."

Mrs. Ferryman's comment stuck with me, and on my way back to number five, I noted again the quaint streets and tiny gardens. A yearning for a quiet life full of friendly neighbors took root. I couldn't do better than Eden Cove.

## The Key Collector's Promise

As if to prove my point, Kenny, accompanied by Liam, Harriet's husband, appeared five minutes after I parked, catching me unloading the car.

"Let us get those for you, Sandra," Liam said.

My arms were happy to let the duo carry the buckets, paintbrushes, rollers, and other supplies. "I appreciate it." I propped open the front door. "Go through to the conservatory and leave it all there."

Liam, compact and muscular, toted two cans in each hand with ease, and Kenny followed suit, but only after clamping a drop cloth under one arm. The boy chattered away to his brother-in-law about some sports team.

I followed them to the conservatory, where Liam put his burden down on the brown tile floor. In my imagination, I could already picture it spiffed up, a cozy spot complete with a floral sofa and pastel throw pillows, a bookcase stuffed with classics, and pots of low-maintenance ivy.

Liam said, "I best get on. I'm due back at work. Kenny can handle it from here." He clapped Kenny on the back.

The boy nodded. "Sure thing." Kenny wasn't as reticent with Liam as he was with me, but I suspected the boy would withdraw into shyness as soon as Liam vacated the scene.

"Ring if you need anything," Liam said.

I thanked him, saw him to the door, and let the dog in.

When I returned to Kenny, I pointed to the bank of windows. "I'd like for you to start on the far left." In a bucket, I found a scraper and handed it to him. "Prep the window casings and woodwork. They don't need much."

He nodded, solemn quietness back in full force.

"I think you have all you need to start." I glanced around the conservatory.

Even barren, the room had a breathtaking view, a great selling point. Advertising copy for such a rental could write itself. Instead of satisfaction at my good fortune in snagging the property, I felt a pinch of jealousy toward my unknown future tenants. Which was silly.

The dog sniffed around and licked a paintbrush.

I eyed the ragamuffin ball of fur. "Come on, pup. Let's put you outside."

Kenny retrieved the paintbrush and set it on a chair. Bending down, he rubbed the dog's face. "He's not bothering anything. I'll put him out if he gets in the way."

My heart softened. So, the boy could talk.

I said, "Don't let him get underfoot."

"I won't." For a fleeting moment, Kenny's eyes met mine before skittering away. "Maybe you should name him."

Name him? I couldn't get attached. What would happen to the dog when I left? I'd posted found dog notices in the village, but no one had responded yet.

Kenny touched noses with the dog and got a lick to the cheek, provoking the first full smile I'd seen on the boy's face. "He looks like an Oscar."

My heart squeezed. If the dog wasn't claimed by the time I needed to return to Louisiana, maybe I could convince Kenny's mother to let him keep the dog. Perhaps such an arrangement would be best all around.

"That's a nice name. I'll think about it," I said. "Listen, I have to make some calls. Do as much as you can in here, and I'll check in later. Let me know if you need help."

Kenny hitched up his pants. "Okay."

What the young man lacked in conversational skills, he made up for with his ability to listen and tend to a job. Besides his job at the family bakery, I'd seen him helping Harriet, and from all appearances Jennifer adored him.

I could trust him.

Unlike Harlow.

My gut told me my mother must be in a care home, but after days with no results, the temptation to touch base with Harlow grew stronger. Surely he knew of a private eye in Suffolk, or at least London, but I couldn't bring myself to trust him.

I sighed and went to the entry table, where I'd left the map. With my mother's last known home as a starting point, I drew a circle, locating and noting down the closest facilities first, spiraling outward and making calls as I went. In this way, I wouldn't skip over any.

The circle grew larger and larger, and edginess crept into my telephone voice. I stopped to check on Kenny's progress, which was as slow as my own, not that I minded. Having Kenny in the house kept me from voicing frustration out loud to myself after each unfruitful call, and gave me a reason to take a breather before diving in again.

Then I finally got a lead and bounced on the balls of my feet in a silent happy dance. At Parks Manor outside Springford they had a Ms. Jones with diabetes. Springford, not Summerdale. The receptionist thought the patient was around forty. My mother was forty-three. I double-checked the name with her, and she confirmed before warning me visiting hours ended at five.

"Kenny," I called out. "I need to run an errand. Can you come back tomorrow?" Hurriedly, I folded the map and tucked it into a drawer as Kenny came into the front room. "Go wash up," I told him. "I'll wait."

I retrieved my purse and opened the door. The dog shot out.

*Silly dog.*

When this was all over, I'd miss him.

By the time I stepped outside, the dog was near the street, his front paws on the knee of a crouching man clad in faded blue jeans and a short-sleeved chambray shirt. A sweet scene, I thought, until my gaze focused. My heart leapt into my throat. I knew that man.

Conner.

## Chapter Fourteen

*May 30, MONDAY Cont.*

"Dog! Come!"

The dog ignored me, scampering in circles around Conner as the man gazed up at me, his impassive brown eyes revealing nothing.

The wayward mutt sniffed Conner's battered cowboy boots while I stood there with my mouth hanging open. After a beat, I came to my senses and snapped my jaws shut before a fly could buzz down my throat. The instinct to slam the door and lock it almost won out, but what good would that do? Conner wasn't going to vanish simply because I didn't want to see him. I'd have to deal with it.

I bit out, "Did Daddy send you?"

"I came on my own." His reply was unhurried and untroubled.

On his own? Not likely.

In a show of bravado, I crossed my arms and looked down my nose at him. "Why are you here?"

Kenny came up and stood next to me. "Who's this?"

"A person I worked with before."

Conner winced and put a hand to the side of his neck. "I came to find you."

My gaze flicked to the street, and Conner looked over his shoulder. Harriet maneuvered a pram through her front garden and hustled toward us. If she'd been a porcupine, every quill would be bristling, ready to fly.

Without slowing her approach, she called out, "Everything all right?" She narrowed her eyes at Conner, and then glanced at me in question.

Amy, the older lady from number four next door, stepped outside, walking stick in hand. For a long time, she fiddled with her doorknob, and then slowly made her way to observe the giant sycamore tree, where a young father with a small child joined her. The child, a girl, dug in the dirt with a plastic shovel, but I had the distinct impression the young father and Amy were keeping a sharp eye on the situation.

Bolstered by the neighbors' presence, I lifted my chin and called to Harriet louder than necessary. "It's fine."

Conner grunted, clearly annoyed at having an audience. "Can you call off the pack?"

Kenny drew himself to his full, skinny height, and stepped closer to my side. A strong wind could blow him over. He was no match for Conner, a former LSU football player, but he had guts.

I lifted my chin higher.

Conner said, "Sandra, I'm here to help. You took off without telling anyone where you were headed."

"Then how did you know where to find me?"

"Come on. You took the property listings and brochures about England from your bulletin board, and then suddenly bought a mysterious property without disclosing the location. You talk about coming to England to find your mother all the time."

True. But still. I eyed him suspiciously.

Harriet waited at the end of the low stone wall dividing my front garden from Amy's and bounced the pram. Poor Jennifer's head bobbled.

The curious tot pointed at Conner. "Who, Mummy? Who?"

Harriet, keeping her attention on Conner, gave Jennifer a squeaky toy.

Conner raked a hand through his thick hair, and it bushed out wolfman style. "Listen. You have it wrong. I'm worried and wanted to help, whatever's going on."

Gripping my elbows, I kept my arms folded tight across my chest and remained silent, ignoring both my distrust of Conner's motives and the desire to take him into confidence. I also ignored the tiny pout of his lips, an unconscious expression he often wore when he felt misunderstood.

Brows knit in frustration, he said, "Can I give you the number to my hotel room?"

Harriet sniffed.

Indifferent to Harriet's disdain, Conner leveled his gaze at me. "I don't know what's going on, but things aren't right at the office, and I'd bet my last dollar you're at the center of it."

At this, Harriet tipped her head to the side, trying to puzzle out who Conner was to me, a question I didn't know the answer to myself. I willed myself not to squirm. Was he as innocent as he made himself out to be?

After fishing a card from his front shirt pocket, he held it out. "We need to talk. Call me."

I didn't approach. He laid the card on top of the low stone wall near my rose bush, strode to a small blue car parked on the street, got in, and drove away.

Amy strolled toward the church, no doubt starting one of her walks. The man chased the little girl, who ran, full-tilt toward the duck pond. The atmosphere felt eerily calm, like the eye of a storm, and I stood right in the middle of it.

Harriet jiggled the pram, and Jennifer giggled, breaking the spell. Kenny crossed the street to Harriet's house and went in.

Stepping forward, I snatched the card and peered at it. Greton Hall, down the way from Sycamore Street. Fancy digs. If anyone could finagle a room at a luxury hotel during the summer on short notice, it was Conner.

But how had he found me, really?

Harlow. It had to be.

After seeing Conner face to face, it was hard to consider him a serious suspect. But if it were as easy to find me as Conner claimed, who else might be on my trail? The hairs on the back of my neck prickled.

Anyone could be watching me.

"You all right?" Harriet asked.

I scrubbed at my forehead as if I could wipe the frightening thoughts from my mind. "I'm fine. So sorry to have involved you."

"Don't worry about it."

Compelled to downplay the interaction and put a period on it, I said, "Me and Conner…it's complicated."

Harriet snorted. "Isn't it always?"

I shifted gears. "I've got a lead on my mother from a care home."

"That's good news!"

"I was about to drive over and see if it's her. They said I had to be there before five." I hesitated.

"Go!" Harriet made a shooing motion. "You can tell me all about it when you get back. Either way. Promise you'll come over?"

I nodded and got into the Renault. And then the stupid thing wouldn't start.

Harriet watched me get out of the car, her face scrunched in sympathy. She looked ready to cry.

I didn't want to know how I looked.

This day had been too much. I needed to go check on the lead. And, apparently, rent a different car. Rick could keep his hunk of junk. Until then, I'd have to depend on another mode of transport. Buses ran several times a day to and from Eden Cove. If I had a ride to the stop, I could catch the hourly, but I'd never get there in time on foot.

"Harriet, can you drive me to the bus stop?"

"Of course I can!" She lit up, as if I'd solved a problem for her, rather than the other way around.

After slinging a diaper bag into her dark blue Ford Escort and buckling Jennifer in, Harriet slid behind the wheel.

"Thanks for this," I said from the passenger's seat, trying to convince myself we could make it.

"No problem." Craning her neck to see behind her, Harriet hit the gas and neatly backed the car into the street, then got us going in the right direction in a blink. As we zipped along, I gripped the door handle, second-guessing my idea of having Harriet try to catch the bus while Jennifer crowed from her car seat in the back. Despite Harriet's best efforts, the only thing I caught was the sight of the red bus receding in the distance.

Harriet grimaced. "Too late." She pulled over.

I said, "I could ask Rick again if he could hurry with the Renault repair."

Skepticism rolled off Harriet in waves. "You could, I suppose."

"I have a terrible premonition. I should go to the care home, but…"

"Does this have anything to do with the guy who showed up at your house?"

Deflecting, I peered out the window. "I'm afraid no one at the care home will talk to me if I arrive after visiting hours. The woman on the phone was quite clear." I chewed my thumbnail. I could try anyway. Find a place to rent a car, or take the late bus and hope.

"Tell you what. I'll take you round." She patted my knee.

"But it's forty minutes away. Are you sure?"

"Of course I'm sure. Can't stand between a girl and her mum." She twisted around and pitched her voice high, talking to Jennifer. "Right, Jen?"

"Right!" Jennifer parroted, yelling and thumping her feet against the back of my seat.

I'm sure Harriet had better things to do than truck me around, but she'd made room for me, taking on my trouble as if it were her own, a kindness I didn't deserve.

My throat clogged, and all I could manage was a strained response. "Thank you, Harriet."

"Think nothing of it. It will be an adventure." Harriet put the car in gear. "Better than washing nappies and scrubbing out sippy cups."

## Chapter Fifteen

*May 30, MONDAY 4:00 P.M.*

Parks Manor had a tiny garden area with benches, and Jennifer made a beeline for it the minute Harriet put her down. The toddler squatted near a fountain, the hem of her dress ruffle brushing the ground. Delicately, she picked a pebble from the grass and ran to Harriet, depositing the gift in her mother's open palm.

"What's this, love?" Harriet cooed.

"Rock. I get more."

Jennifer ran back to the same spot and got another pebble and the game continued, Harriet making much of it.

I had no memories of such moments with my mother, yet here I was, about to come crashing into her world. Not that I had a choice.

"I'm going in," I said.

"Should I stay out here with Jen for a bit?"

"It might be best. Come into the lobby when she gets tired."

Harriet gave a thumbs-up.

The cozy, welcoming lobby was all pastels and potted plants. A young receptionist sat behind a desk, staring at a computer monitor.

"Excuse me," I said. "I'm here to visit Iris Jones?"

The pale young woman looked up, tucking her ink-black hair behind one ear. "Who?"

I repeated the name and she tapped a few keys.

"Nobody here by that name."

She sounded bored.

I exhaled loudly. "I just called. Iris Jones, forty-three. She's diabetic. I called just this afternoon and was told I could come see her."

"I'm sorry." She shrugged. "There's no one currently registered under that name."

"Did she leave?"

"I'm not authorized to give out that information. You could talk to the facility supervisor."

"All right. May I speak with him?"

"He's left for the day. You can try again tomorrow." She opened a drawer, took out a package of gum and unwrapped a piece, pausing to frown at me. "Anything else I can help you with?" She popped the gum into her mouth.

I looked at the ceiling, then back to her blank face. This one wasn't going to provide me a crumb. I'd find someone else to help.

"That's all. Thanks."

*For nothing.*

A young woman in a smock carrying a bouquet of daisies walked past me and straight through a set of double doors leading deeper into the facility.

## The Key Collector's Promise

The rooms must be down there. If nothing else, I could ask other residents about Iris. I was halfway through the doors when the bored young receptionist let out a squawk.

"You can't go in there without checking in! I told you your person wasn't here."

A burly male attendant in white materialized. "Help you, miss?"

"I was only seeing what was down here." My defenses rose, along with an uncomfortable blush. I wasn't in the wrong here, but these people made me feel as if I'd stumbled into a private party, uninvited. "I was told earlier today my..." I flailed about for a suitable word, "relative, Iris Jones, was here."

"Room number?"

"I don't know."

The young receptionist joined us. "I told her the lady she wants to see isn't registered." Hands on hips, she glared at me.

It shouldn't be this hard.

The adrenaline powering me drained away, leaving me exhausted. I had the urge to plop down in the middle of the hall and sit there until they told me where Iris was. "I just need to find her."

The young receptionist bit her lip and looked to the attendant, who seemed more comfortable in his role, not as new on the job as the gum-chewing girl.

In the patient voice health workers often used with skittish people, he said, "Perhaps you got the wrong care home?"

"I wrote down the name and address." I dug in my purse, fished out the rumpled scrap of paper, and pointed to the writing. "Here it is. And I called right before I came."

"I'm sure we can get it sorted, but if your relative isn't in the system, Bonnie here is correct. You'll have better luck tomorrow, when the director is here."

Better luck tomorrow. He wasn't any more use than the gum-chewer, Bonnie.

I crossed my arms. "Not two hours ago I was told Iris was here. Can't we deal with this now?"

He acted like he hadn't heard me. "Wait here a moment. I'll get some brochures containing our policies and details."

At least ten minutes passed before a very young lady, clearly a volunteer by her striped smock, tentatively approached me. She held out a couple of shiny brochures. "I was meant to give these to you?"

No point in getting annoyed at this girl.

I forced a smile and took the offered materials. "Thank you. I'm trying to locate my mum, Iris Jones. Do you know her?"

She shook her head. "Sorry, I don't."

I gave her my phone number anyway.

Now what? Force my way in? Not that I would ever do such a thing. Frustrated and fuming at my ineptitude, I adjusted the strap of my handbag and strode toward the lobby.

Tucked into a corner chair, Harriet held a sleepy Jennifer in her lap. The child lolled against her like a rag doll.

"No luck. They say she's not here."

"What?" Absently, Harriet stroked Jennifer's tangled hair.

I perched on a chair. "I'm absolutely sure the woman I talked to on the phone said they had a Jones here. Maybe she was wrong, but I'll have to come back tomorrow on my own to find out for certain."

## The Key Collector's Promise

"That's a long way we came." Harriet rose to her feet and shifted a whining Jennifer. "All right, grizzle-bear. Not much longer now."

I stood, ready to leave, but Harriet said, "You wait right here. Don't move."

She strode to the desk and addressed the receptionist, or tried to, over Jennifer's complaints. I couldn't see Harriet's expression, but her posture exuded self-assurance. Less than ten minutes later, she did an about face and approached me.

"There is a Ms. Jones on the rehab side, but no one can see her right now. Call back in tomorrow. She should be back in her regular room by then and be able to receive visitors."

"What? How did you find out?" I stared at her, amazed. And I thought I had persuasive skills. They were nothing compared to Harriet's.

"I told her I'd stand there until she found someone who could tell me what happened to Ms. Jones. The Ms. Jones we had driven all the way from Eden Cove to inquire after." Harriet swayed and patted Jennifer's back. "Once I sat the diaper bag on the counter, she didn't seem keen on me staying long." She smirked.

Now that she'd mentioned it, I noticed the bag had a distinct odor.

"Harriet! Is there a dirty diaper in there?"

Her face crinkled up in a delightfully wicked grin. "I've had practice dealing with her sort." She passed me a folded paper. "I asked for the details."

Hands shaking, I unfolded it and read the name, Iris Jones, dietary restrictions for any foods brought in for her, and the date she'd return to the facility, tomorrow. "Harriet, you are an angel. This means so much to me."

Blushing, Harriet turned away and dropped a kiss on Jennifer's cheek. "Come on. Let's get this one settled in the car after I find a bin to stow the smelly nappy. We can grab takeaway on the trip home."

Halfway back to Eden Cove, Harriet wheeled through a drive-through burger joint. "Burgers and fries, that's what you like, right?"

"Sure." I could've done fish and chips but didn't want to sound like a tourist. "I'm paying."

"No, you're not."

I injected a plaintive note into my voice. "Please, Harriet. Let me do this for you."

Jennifer echoed me. "Pwease." She matched my pathos, if not my pronunciation.

Harriet laughed. "Fine, then."

We parked to eat.

I took a huge, cheesy bite of greasy goodness, and my eyes rolled back into my head. "This is wonderful." Always counting calories, I hadn't had the pleasure of a fried beef patty on a bun in months. I licked ketchup off my thumb. "This was a great idea, Harriet."

"I'm glad. We make a pretty good team."

"Team? You saved the day at the care home single-handedly, no teamwork about it."

"I guess I owed you for Kenny."

"What do you mean?"

"He's been locking horns with Dad, teenage stuff. School's been hard as well. He's been at loose ends but has perked up since you've come. He goes on about you. Thank you for being a safe place for him."

# The Key Collector's Promise

Me? A safe place? Not really. The weight of what she'd said pressed on me. I'd been nice, but hadn't gone out of my way. Not really.

I swallowed my bite of food past the lump in my throat. "He's a big help."

Jennifer had fallen fast asleep, leaving Harriet and me to eat in companionable silence, save for the radio turned low to Boy George crooning about time. I'd never be able to get back lost time with my mother. Maybe she didn't care about the lost years. Maybe she preferred the past to stay hidden.

Misgivings ballooned in my chest until I felt ready to explode, and I blurted out, "My mother doesn't know I'm coming. What if she won't see me?"

"Surely she will." Harriet patted my knee.

The hole Iris had left in my life hurt, and being physically so much closer to her left me aching and scared. Sure, I was here to warn her, but was it terrible I wanted more? Old demons circled, whispering.

Why had Iris let me go? If she'd had a good reason, she could've contacted me if she'd wanted to.

"What if she'd rather I hadn't come?"

Harriet passed me an extra napkin. "You must keep the faith. She'll see how much you care, coming so far to see her."

I wiped my nose and sniffed.

A worry crease appeared between Harriet's brows. She examined my face. "You'll be all right coming back tomorrow on your own?"

I forced a shaky laugh. "Of course. Don't worry over me. Tomorrow I'll be my old self. Today my nerves are shot from all the surprises."

"I guess you could say so. Surprises like a guy from Louisiana?" With a knowing look, Harriet popped a fried potato into her mouth. She wouldn't pry, but a healthy curiosity had come to roost.

I shrugged, noncommittal, my stress level shooting back up. When Conner had shown up at the terraced house, he'd claimed to be worried about me. Could I believe him? Maybe. After all, he was the same guy who, when Addie had a cold, made her hot honeyed tea unasked.

But the man had a tendency to keep his private thoughts private. And he wasn't going away. It would be helpful to have the neighbors alerting me.

I said, "Let me know if you see Conner around again. He can be persistent. Doesn't know how to let things go."

The half-eaten burger sat in my lap, and I wrapped it up, appetite gone.

Jennifer wriggled and made a snuffling noise, our cue to get back on the road. I silently thanked her for putting an end to the conversation.

If only the questions plaguing me about Conner were as easy to quell.

## Chapter Sixteen

*May 31, TUESDAY 2:00 A.M.*

I woke in the middle of the night, disoriented, and sat upright on the air mattress I was using for a bed in the smaller of the two upstairs bedrooms. Thunder rumbled and wind rattled the panes of the windows, moaning as if it wanted in.

Oscar, *Dog*, I reminded myself, burrowed into my side. During the night, he'd abandoned his cushion at the foot of the bed and crawled in with me. Lightening flickered through the darkness, punctuated by a crack of thunder, sending my throat into spasms. I startled so bad, it was a wonder I didn't end up on the floor. The dog didn't like it either and whined, which exasperated me. Wasn't he supposed to protect me?

I nudged him with my toe. "It's only a storm." He pressed closer.

Downstairs, something crashed. My pulse rocketed, and I scrambled out of bed, plastering myself to the wall. I listened.

Nothing.

It hadn't been nothing a minute ago. Waves of hot and cold washed over my entire body. Light-headed, I clung to the wall. Why, oh why hadn't I gotten a phone for the jack upstairs?

In such a small house, there was nowhere to hide. I was a sitting duck, waiting for an intruder to come after me.

Creeping across the room in my bare feet, I cast about for a weapon and grabbed a bedside lamp, winding the cord around the skinny base.

No sound came from the house, save normal creaks and groans. I moved toward the door and stopped, listening so hard my ears rang.

A hairy something brushed my ankle. I shrieked and whirled around holding the lamp aloft, ready to bash the brains out of any lurking monster.

The dog pressed against my naked ankle again.

I silently stamped my foot and hissed, "Oscar!"

He bristled, but not at me. He stared out my open bedroom door, a low growl rumbling in his chest. Then he darted over the threshold and shot down the stairs, with me stumbling after him.

Slowing at the last step, I strained to see in the dark. Rain beat against the house, and the sound of a seaside storm wasn't relaxing at all, not in this case. With both hearing and vision diminished, I took a few tentative steps into the front room, promptly whacking my shin on the old couch. With a yelp, I lost hold of the lamp. It thumped to the floor while I simultaneously dropped to a crouch. My fingers felt around and closed on the cord. I dragged the lamp close, reestablishing my grip on the base. From my hiding place behind the couch, I waited, heart hammering in my ears.

Nothing. Nobody there.

## The Key Collector's Promise

Oscar licked my face. I batted him away.

By now, any lurking bad guy could've found me easily enough. Time to flip on the lights and end this foolishness. I stood, senses tuned for anything amiss, but all seemed normal.

*See? No lurking murderer. Just a storm. You're okay.*

The self-pep talk helped, but I kept a tight hold on the lamp, waving it like a batter ready to strike, as I jumped into each room and turned on lights until the place blazed. The dog trotted after me, unimpressed by my caution.

A branch stuck through one of the conservatory windows, and I wilted with relief. Like I'd thought. Just the storm. A gust of wind rattled the broken pane and rain spattered in, wetting the tile floor.

"Silly dog." I shook my head. "Look at us. Scared of the wind."

I'd have to fasten plastic over the window until I could have it repaired. How much would a replacement cost? I mentally tallied up my cash on hand. A trip to the bank would delay my return to Parks Manor.

Distracted, tired, and more than a little annoyed, I shuffled to the kitchen for plastic trash bags. They'd have to do until morning.

I got a trash bag from under the sink, turned around, and froze. A paper, folded in half, sat in the center of the kitchen table. Had I left the paper there? I didn't think so.

My fingers went numb.

Oscar came into the kitchen, nails clicking on the linoleum floor, and the ordinary action unstuck me. I told myself it must be a note from Kenny I'd overlooked. Nothing nefarious. After all, this wasn't the big city. It was Eden Cove.

Still, when I reached for the note, the white noise of angry waves flinging themselves against the coastline beat in my head.

I unfolded the paper. Large, blocky letters scrawled across a page.

*SHHHH*

The letter writer had found me. The letter writer was here.

In the house.

The tang of electric fear filled my mouth. Cold wind slapped my cheeks, and I looked up, saw the kitchen door moving with the breeze.

It was gaping wide open.

## Chapter Seventeen

*May 31, TUESDAY 2:15 A.M.*

In my head, Addie's voice urged me to get out, and I sprinted for the front door, or maybe the phone, I wasn't sure which. The dog was too close, underfoot, and I tripped, careening into a wall and bouncing off, not stopping or even pausing as I burst from my door and tore down the street, yelling at the top of my lungs.

I hammered Harriet's door.

Liam answered, wearing boxers and a white T-shirt, his stocky form filling the entryway.

"Someone's in my house! Let me in!" I pushed my way past him and halted, my breathing hard and jagged.

Harriet rushed to us, her face ghost white. "In your house? Are you hurt?" She drew me deeper into the house. The warm, dry house. Safe.

"I'm not hurt," I said. Tears streaked my cheeks, and I wiped them with unsteady hands.

Liam picked up a cricket bat. "I'll go over."

"No!" Harriet and I both yelled at the same time.

Harriet took the bat. "Call the police."

Upstairs, Jennifer cried for her mum.

Harriet grabbed me by the shoulders. "Was it that fellow?"

"What?"

Her grip tightened, fingernails digging in. "The fellow who came around to your house."

"Conner? No. That's ridiculous!"

Harriet shot me a look, but let go.

"No." I repeated, emphatically shaking my head. "He'd never."

Doubts snaked into my thoughts, and I knew my expression betrayed me. I wasn't sure. Perhaps Daddy had sent him to keep an eye on me, but Conner wouldn't scare me, would he? Unless Daddy was the one trying to keep me quiet and thought I'd blab or cause trouble from over the ocean. I pressed my cold fingertips against my temples.

Harriet lasered in on me, ignoring Jennifer's crying.

The doorbell rang.

Jennifer's cries took on a note of hysteria, and Harriet's attention wavered from me. She went to the door and let in the silver-haired lady, my next door neighbor. "Come in, Amy. I've got to get Jen."

I suddenly felt guilty. Too intent on saving my own skin, I hadn't spared a thought for the elderly lady on the other side of my wall.

I said, "Are you all right?"

"Perfectly fine." Calm as could be, she tightened the sash of her silk robe, then offered her hand. "I'm Amy Lewis. From number four."

## The Key Collector's Promise

The normal, every-day gesture had a calming effect on the situation, and my jack-rabbit pulse slowed its frantic rhythm. If we were doing niceties, it couldn't be the end of the world.

Tentative, I placed my trembling hand in her firm grasp and cleared my throat. "Sandra, number five."

Her palm was warm, her grip comforting, the handshake one of a capable woman.

For sure she'd heard me screaming blue murder and had been rousted out of bed. A wave of gratefulness for terrace houses, thin walls, and a packed-tight village street swamped me.

Liam had the police on the line. I sketched out what had happened, listing the facts. At my mention of finding the back door open, Liam squared his shoulders and puffed out his chest, ready to take on the intruders, while Harriet, with a sleepy Jennifer propped on her hip, locked her own front door, and peered out the narrow side window.

The new note burned a hole in my pocket, but I did as it said, keeping my mouth shut about that.

# Chapter Eighteen

*May 31, TUESDAY 2:30 A.M.*

Harriet and I watched out her front window, waiting for the police to arrive. Amy and Liam had tea in the kitchen. How they could remain so unruffled in the circumstances—while I chewed three of my nails to the quick and worked up a good stress sweat—remained a mystery to me.

Several police cars arrived on the street, their lights flashing, and I felt a little better. Anyone around would either hightail it out of there or get caught. Because of our view, I couldn't see when the officers entered number five, but they headed towards it.

A lone officer, young, male, and baby-faced, approached Harriet's door. We waited for the knock, and then she ushered him to the front room and we all sat down, Harriet and I on the couch with the officer opposite in an armchair. A damp Oscar lay his head on top of my foot.

Pen poised over a small black notebook, the baby-faced officer said, "I read the intake information, but need to ask a

## The Key Collector's Promise

few questions. Did you see anyone?" Gray eyes gazed at me from under the brim of a police officer's cap.

"No. I didn't." I explained what happened as he jotted notes.

"And you don't know of anyone who would want to harm you? Any unusual characters been hanging about?"

Anyone who wanted to harm me? No. Not me. My mother.

Harriet opened her mouth as if to speak, no doubt to mention Conner, but I clamped down on her thigh, and she shut up.

The man waited for an answer.

My insides quivering, I picked up a baby toy from the couch, a soft, yellow, donut-shape, and kneaded it. "No one wants to hurt me. No one I know of."

It was true. Whoever had sent either note hadn't threatened my person. But the idea of Daddy being behind the entire escapade wasn't beyond imagining, and the unadorned truth turned the air in my lungs to ice.

The officer closed his notebook. "Even after you get the all clear, I suggest staying elsewhere for the rest of the night. Get the window fixed as soon as possible, and always secure the locks. If you remember anything or have concerns, call right away." He handed me a business card. "In future, if someone tries to enter or you hear suspicious noises while you're home alone, call 999."

With a mouth as dry as cotton, I said, "Thank you." The yellow toy squeaked in my grip, and I put it down.

Amy had a hushed conversation with the officer and departed, returning to her house, I assumed. She'd probably be glad to see the back of me when I left Eden Cove and peace returned to the neighborhood.

The minute the officer took his leave, Harriet turned on me, hands on hips. "Shouldn't you have at least mentioned the guy, Conner? I know you're running from someone. Is it him?"

"Conner wouldn't hurt me."

Would he? I was so confused and tired. And scared. What if it were Conner? He was in the area. Had he left the note?

No. Not possible.

I shook my head. "I don't think he had anything to do with it."

Unless it was all about Strickland, keeping me in line for the next ten days until the deal went through. Feeling sick to my bones, I banished the thought of Conner resorting to such tactics.

Attempting a scoff, I said, "Surely it was someone who thought the place was empty. Or a horrible prank. Rick told me of such goings on."

"A prank?" Harriet pinched her lips closed tight. She inhaled through her nose, then let out a breath and said, "In any event, you're staying the night here. Liam can go across and get a change of clothes and anything else you need."

"Thank you." I blinked back tears. I'd be safe here, with Harriet and Liam.

On the heels of relief, a thought popped into my head. What if there were clues left behind? Clues only I would see as such?

I had to go see.

"I'd better go over with Liam. He wouldn't know what to get." I forced a grin, just to prove I wasn't scared. "Plus, I'd rather pick out my own underthings, you know."

Harriet played along, ready to let go of the dark possibilities I'd brought into her quiet street. She matched my tone with a wry, amused one. "All right."

Fake bravery aside, I stayed glued to Liam as he strode to my house, the bat resting on his solid shoulder.

At number five, all was quiet. Other than the broken window and the lamp-turned-bat I'd abandoned, no items seemed missing or out of place. My passport, money, the original letter, and Harlow's file remained secure, locked in my luggage, much to my relief.

## Chapter Nineteen

*May 31, TUESDAY Morning*

The next morning, I sat at Harriet's table with Liam and Kenny, and took mouse-sized nibbles of toast between sips of tea. Jennifer had already breakfasted and was getting a bath. Sporting a magnificent case of bedhead, Kenny shoveled down cocoa cereal. I hadn't even realized he'd been staying over. Apparently, he'd slept through the whole episode.

Around a mouthful, he said, "I can come over to number five with you."

"Not a good idea." For the umpteenth time, I checked my watch. I'd called a car rental service, not Rick, and they would soon deliver a car to my house, and I needed to meet the window repair guy over there.

Kenny scowled, the first time he'd done so at something I'd said.

Liam ruffled Kenny's hair, and the scowl deepened. "I'll go over with her, mate, and meet with the glazier. He's a friend of mine."

## The Key Collector's Promise

I was glad Liam knew the glazier. I didn't relish the idea of letting a stranger into the house.

Kenny clammed up, whether from his normal behavior or pique at being left out, I couldn't figure out, and I left Harriet's house wishing he hadn't been unhappy. I'd gotten attached to the teen.

The rest of the morning unfolded smoothly enough. The car arrived on time, and the glazier shortly after, though the glazier, a stranger, simply being there made me fidgety as a feline.

It helped to know my closest neighbors were on high alert, and I was grateful for them. Besides, even with a closer look, no evidence of an intruder remained. Everything seemed so normal, and in the clear light of day, I could almost convince myself the letter I'd found at the office and the note left on my table in Eden Cove were written by two different hands.

After the glazier finished, packed his tools, and gave a cheery wave, Liam made as if to follow the guy out, but I stopped him.

I said, "Have other people reported similar events to what happened last night?" I'd breathe easier if they had. No doubt most, if not all, of Sycamore Street had heard about the break-in by now.

Liam frowned. "There's been a few instances of broken flower pots, gates left open, rolling rubbish bins at midnight, that sort of thing." He pulled on his earlobe, thinking. "If it was those boys, I'd like to give them a piece of my mind. Opening doors is going too far. Best to play it safe. Get new locks. And keep your wits about you."

"I will."

I let him go, wishing I could keep stocky, calm Liam and his cricket bat by my side in case I encountered trouble on my way to Parks Manor.

By midmorning, I arrived at Park's Manor Care Home. The facility's security measures and adherence to visiting hours no longer frustrated me, rather, they eased my mind.

A different receptionist sat behind the desk. I told her I was a relative of Iris's.

She pointed to a cup of pens. "Fill out the visitor's book."

Obediently, I scribbled my first name, then hesitated and used my middle name as a last name. I said, "Iris had been moved when I came by last. What room is she in?"

"Thirty-two."

Her watching eyes bored a hole in the back of my head until the double doors closed behind me. The same male orderly who'd ditched me the day before pushed an elderly lady in a wheelchair. He acknowledged me with a curt nod, no smile. I'd better be on my best behavior or they'd boot me out.

Scuff marks marred the shiny beige floor. Unlike the outdoor garden and the lobby, no other color broke up the plain-as-rice-pudding hall, and the further I walked, the smaller I felt. I hoped the residents' living quarters had more personality, but resisted peeking in the open doors. Televisions blared from a couple of rooms but in others, snatches of conversation reassured me residents had more than TV programs to occupy them.

I counted down the rooms.

*Thirty-one.*
*Thirty-two.*
*Thirty-three.*

At Iris's door, I came to a halt and dabbed sweat from my upper lip, wishing I'd put on extra deodorant. I tapped on the door.

A young brunette woman in blue jeans and a pastel striped blouse peeked out, then swung the door open wide. "Did you bring the menu?"

"I, um. No."

She waved me in. "It doesn't matter. You can take Mum's order anyway."

Mum? I checked the number of the door. Thirty-three. Had I heard the receptionist wrong?

The young woman retreated into the room, and I took a step forward. "I don't think…"

She sat down beside a bed. My gaze drifted to the middle-aged woman lying there, her eyes nearly closed, and a jolt of recognition shot through me. The hair wasn't the same corn-silk yellow, but I knew the shape of her jaw, her sleepy smile. The young woman took my mother's unresisting hand and looked at me, expectant.

My mother sighed, inhaled. Drugged? It seemed so.

The young woman shot me a puzzled look.

I shifted on my feet. This wasn't what I'd expected. She'd called Iris Mum.

I said, "Umm. I'm not on staff here."

The girl's rosy complexion and dark brunette hair were nothing like my mother's or mine. And she was curvy and short. Was she the right age to be Iris's daughter? My mum had me at seventeen. Daddy had taken me to America when I was four. There was no sister.

Not then.

The truth dawned on me. Mum had gone on with life. Of course she had. But another child?

I'd been replaced.

Sharp pain sliced through me, as if the betrayal was fresh, not a lifetime old, and I shoved the thought aside. Tears had no place here, with this stranger.

*Swallow it. Toughen up. Focus on your mission.*

"I have an urgent message for Iris."

Iris mustered for a moment, gazing blearily at me before giving up and sinking back into her pillows.

"She's not up for conversation." With a half-smirk, the young woman gave the kind of eye rolls teenagers bestow on adults. She was younger than she first appeared. Not a teen, but young. "But you can tell me. Or come back tomorrow when Mum is feeling better."

She smoothed the bed cover, the smirk softening into a patient smile. Acting the way a daughter would act.

A sister.

I couldn't wrap my head around it. Wouldn't Harlow have found out if I had a sister?

Before I could make a total fool of myself, I blurted out, "I came to tell her about an important letter."

The girl's eyebrows rose in interest. "Did Mum win something?"

This wasn't going well. I needed to talk straight to my mother, but her face was lax and her mouth hung open. Asleep.

My stomach knotted. Bolting, no matter how much I wanted to, wasn't an option.

*Just tell this person to be on the lookout. Fall apart later if you have to, in private.*

## The Key Collector's Promise

My realtor persona clicked into place. "I wish it was something of that nature, but no. No prize."

How to explain to this girl? I wasn't going to tell her I was possibly her sister. Iris should do that. My throat grew tight, and I swallowed hard.

I could do this.

I was Sandra Lejeune, and had handled plenty of tough customers.

*Be direct. Be concise.*

"I can't divulge details until I can speak with her directly, but there's an issue of concern. A personal safety issue. Your mother should be on the alert. Watch out for anything unusual and notify security if any strangers approach."

"Strangers? Like you?" The young woman's dark eyes sparkled with amusement, but the comment jabbed.

"It's not a joke. Trust me." At my harsh tone, her lighthearted attitude fled.

She narrowed her eyes until they were barely more than slits and inched her chair closer to my mother's bed. "You're not on staff. You said so yourself. I think you better leave."

Great. Now I'd antagonized the girl. Or worse, frightened her, although she didn't look frightened. I backed out of the room.

The hall was a blur, as was the lobby, and the walk to the car. How I found the rental car, I'll never know, but I did. I sat there, numb, for ten or fifteen minutes, maybe longer.

My mother had another daughter. One she held hands with. One who knew all about her.

I didn't even know my mother's favorite color.

Like an idiot, I started crying. I'd been replaced, but what had I expected?

The worst thing about the whole situation was that I still needed to make sure my mother got the warning. The girl wasn't likely to tell her, or if she did, the story would be about a weirdo spouting vague warnings.

My nose dripped. I opened the glove box. No tissue. Searched my purse. None there, either. I cried into my sleeve and pounded the steering wheel. Look at me, so unprepared I hadn't a Kleenex. How was I to rescue anyone? Not to mention, my mum didn't know me when I stood right in front of her. I had to get away from here, from these people I didn't know and who didn't know me.

After a time fumbling with the keys, I finally fitted them into the ignition slot, cranked the engine, and got out of there.

---

I wasn't ready to face the watchful neighbors of number five when I got to Eden Cove, so I took the road to the old church, St. Bartholomew.

The minute I opened the car door, the perfume of roses rushed me, a salt breeze carrying the scent from the large garden beyond the church. It smelled like joy and grief intermingled.

Fitting.

My bruised spirit churned. What right had I to feel betrayed? I should have known she wasn't the type to mope around pining for a lost daughter. Daddy had told me about her. Iris had been unfaithful to him, impulsive. Untrustworthy.

I walked the garden, hoping my agitation would fade. If I could let cold logic take over, my focus would be on my mission, not my hurt. I felt vulnerable and needed to protect my heart. Whether from my flesh and blood mother or my tender, unexamined fantasies of a mother and daughter reconciliation wasn't clear, but one thing was obvious. My childish, storybook imaginings weren't going to survive a collision with reality. Dreams were only safe as long as you never took the chance to make them real. But what use was an unrealized dream?

A mass of white flowers tumbled over a stone wall, and a riot of pink blooms played peek-a-boo, hiding in them. Plants filled every space along the walking path.

These flowers, fresh and new, had emerged from roots decades old, perhaps older. I fingered my necklace with its key, wondering about my own roots. It would've pleased Daddy if my transplant from England to the States had been complete, cutting off emotional ties to the UK. Perhaps my mother felt the same way. Perhaps I'd sensed it all along, and that was why it had taken this threat to send me back to my birthplace.

I wandered, isolated from the world, turning over my private hurts and unsure how to feel about it all, until I happened upon Mrs. Ferryman sitting on a stone bench, her eyes closed, her face to the sun. It surprised me to see anyone else around, though I don't know why, and I stepped back, meaning to leave her in peace.

Remaining as she was, face to the sun, she said, "Lovely day for roses. This time of year brings out the best blooms. It's always so peaceful here." She opened her eyes and smiled.

It was a restful smile. Not what I would expect from the mom of a teen who'd had a rough time of it. Or any teen, for that matter. Maybe the garden had an effect on people. I should drag my air mattress out here.

She gestured to the spot next to her. "Care to sit? There's plenty of room."

Her offer to share the space was a balm I sorely needed after the disturbing night and the day's stressful encounter at Parks Manor.

"Thank you, Mrs. Ferryman."

"Please, call me Grace. We are neighbors."

"Thank you, Grace."

What a pretty name. I had a hard time not adding 'Miss' to the front of it the way we did back home.

Petals littered the bench. I cleared off a spot beside her and, not quite relaxed, perched.

"Few things are as comforting as a flower garden." Her periwinkle eyes twinkled with good humor. "Except for fresh sticky buns or a nice sponge."

A laugh escaped my throat. "I'll keep that in mind."

"Of course, you can always talk to the pastor. I can take you to see him, if you like. He's about the church somewhere."

Embarrassed, I flushed. Did I look so lost I needed leading to church? "I'm fine," I said, lying through my teeth.

"We're here for you, you know."

"I'm fine, really." I tried on a smile.

She made a humming noise in her throat, one indicating she may or may not agree with my declaration. Bending down, she picked up a sad, wilted bloom. "The garden is so peaceful. Sometimes I feel closer to God here, but when we call on Him, He listens to us, no matter where we are."

"I don't go to church much."

"A person doesn't have to be in church to talk to God. He hears His children."

I didn't think that was how it worked. It was one thing asking God to protect my mother, but expecting Him to listen to my hurts about tangled-up relationships? I'd been taught

God wasn't a vending machine. No white-bearded Santa resided in the sky, ready to pass out presents when folks got around to asking. I'd neglected church, too busy working or too tired from work or, if I were honest, out of sheer laziness.

God was probably fed up with me.

Either Mrs. Ferryman was a good guesser, or my thoughts were written all over my face.

She took my clenched fist, teased open my hand, and laid the flower in my palm. "He hears you, Sandra. He always hears."

The fact she knew my name didn't erase my loneliness. I felt alone in unfamiliar seas, and not sure which direction to paddle in.

# Chapter Twenty

*May 31, TUESDAY Evening*

Because of the break-in, I needed new door locks and found what I needed at a shop in the village. I added a savory pie to my purchases, a bribe for the dog because I'd left him cooped up in the back garden too long.

I parked in front of number five. The rosebush in front of the blue-painted home, I noticed, was a sister of one of the varieties in the garden by the church. I got out with my bags.

Liam was wielding a broom, scrubbing the walk in front of number three. When he saw me, he lifted a hand, and I waved back, losing my grip on my purchases. Groceries, locks, and all tumbled to the ground.

Liam propped the broom against the house and jogged over. Wiping his hands on the front of his stained T-shirt, he bent, helping me pick up the dropped purchases. "You doing all right?" He smelled of outdoors and man-sweat, an oddly comforting combination.

"Sure," I said, my voice too loud, almost shrill. I moderated my tone. "I got new locks."

## The Key Collector's Promise

"A good idea, that." He squinted at the second-floor windows. "Want me to do house check? I'm sure it's fine, but I can look if it makes you feel better."

Dog set to barking from the house's back garden. Another layer of protection. If an intruder somehow slipped by the neighbors, surely the dog would raise the alarm. All the same, I welcomed Liam's presence.

"A check would be nice, if you don't mind."

After I let the dog in, I shadowed Liam, and the dog shadowed me. No stranger hid under the bedframe or in a closet. We went back downstairs, and Liam watched me unload the bags I'd left on the entryway table.

He said, "Need help installing those locks?"

I shrugged, starting to feel a little embarrassed at my neediness. "I can do it myself."

Back home, I'd replaced my fair share of locks. Even had my own tools.

Liam rubbed the back of his head. "I'd better install those. Harriet will ask if you're secure, and I can't risk upsetting her, now can I? Be back in a tick with my tools."

Before I could protest, he was already over the threshold.

Once he returned, it took less than an hour to replace the locks.

Liam dropped his screwdriver into the battered green toolbox he'd brought over and snapped the lid shut. "Come for tea. Harriet's making a chicken and some veg."

"I would, but I've got a bad headache." It wasn't a lie.

"Say no more. You should take a rest." A tiny frown line creased the space above his friendly gray eyes. "Is there anything else you need?"

Impulsively, I blurted out, "Do you have a Bible I could borrow?"

Ever since the encounter with Mrs. Ferryman in the rose garden, fragments of Bible verses from my private school days kept popping into my memory, such as, *study to show thyself approved*, and *a bruised reed He will not break*. Which, I supposed, was the purpose of teaching us children memory verses in the first place.

With one forefinger, Liam tapped his toolbox absently. "I'm sure Harriet has one. Let me ask her. I'll be right back, one way or another."

While he was gone, I busied myself. I reheated the pie and cut it in half, then halved it again and minced up the dog's portion, thinking to mix it with kibble.

I recognized Liam's gentle knock when he returned, but peered out the window all the same before opening up. He had a brown Bible in his grasp. I turned the shiny new deadbolt and let him in.

He held out the Bible. "Here you are."

I took it from him. It was soft, with worn corners. "Thank you, Liam. For this, and for being a good neighbor. You don't know how much I appreciate you." My voice cracked. "And Harriet."

Liam's neck turned as red as a chili pepper. "No problem."

This family had gone above and beyond, and I wanted more than anything to look after them in kind. I'd left Kenny alone in the house before, but now regretted what felt like an error in judgement. In fact, he shouldn't be around me at all.

I said, "Listen, Liam, until we know for sure it's safe, I'd rather Kenny didn't come over anymore. The repair work can wait."

"I don't know if you should go so far. No one will prowl about in the daytime. Too many people around."

I could just picture an overeager Kenny taking on an intruder and getting hurt, or worse. My heart rolled over in my chest at the thought of a goon mixing it up with the teen. "I don't want to worry about putting Kenny in harm's way." I'd miss the boy's quiet company, but safety came first. "Tell Harriet," I insisted. "And Mrs. Ferryman. This house is off limits for now."

He put his hands up. "All right, all right. Ring if you need us." He gave an abbreviated wave and let himself out.

I sat on the lumpy couch and opened the Bible, my fingers trailing along the gilt fore-edge of the book and across the words, the onionskin paper as soft as a whisper. We'd had a housekeeper one summer who read the Bible. I'd been too old for a nanny, but she'd read stories to me and baked lemon cookies almost every week. And she sang church songs. What was it she had told me? Always start in the gospels. Or had that been one of my teachers at school? Either way, I opened the Bible and began reading. I needed God and had to get back on track.

The familiar words of Matthew chapter seven, verse seven resonated with me.

*Ask, and it shall be given you; seek, and ye shall find; knock, and it shall be opened unto you. Matthew 7:7 KJV*

That's exactly what I was trying to do, but wrestling a clear set of directions from the King James wasn't as easy as the Sisters had made it out to be. Or was it? If I kept focused on God, sooner or later, I'd find the answers.

I kept reading.

The image of the young woman in my mother's room intruded. The dark-haired girl had called Iris mum, but it could've been a pet name. And if it wasn't?

A pain behind my ribs stole my breath. I clutched the key around my neck and bit my lip hard to hold tears at bay. It was only the stress. Anyone would feel upset. It was nothing. Of course Iris had moved on with her life. What had I expected? Haunting, childhood whispers returned.

*She doesn't want you.*

A wound that never quite healed tore open, and there I was again, a lost girl wanting a mother who never came. The pages of the Bible blurred, and I put the book aside.

I cried myself hoarse while the dog licked my face, whining and nudging me with his cold nose.

When the cryfest ended, I didn't scold myself as I usually did. I didn't wallow. I didn't tell myself I was being ridiculous. Instead, I admitted I hurt and probably would hurt, if not forever, at least for a very long time.

I drank a glass of water. Held a bag of frozen peas to my swollen eyes for five minutes. Then I walked a circuit of the downstairs, closing and securing all but two windows I left open for ventilation. The whole time, Oscar followed close on my heels.

I scratched him on the head. "No one is getting in without making a racket. You bark if you hear anything, okay?"

He wagged his tail, which I took for a yes.

It was the best I could do for now. As for my mother, I'd come to warn her of the threat, and that's what I'd do.

## Chapter Twenty-One

*June 1, WEDNESDAY*

It had been a week and a day since I'd found the letter on the carpet in the office. Seven days in England. For this meeting with Iris, I dressed with care in a cream blouse, dress slacks, and low-heeled pumps. As a final touch, I wore my gold knot earrings.

The morning drive to Parks Manor was nerve-wracking. I felt like I was being watched, and constantly glanced in the rearview mirror. Every time my attention returned to the road, my instincts screamed at me to get in the other lane. During the seconds before my brain kicked in, reminding me I was in England and would not smash into oncoming traffic, my heart must've stopped ten times.

At a store along the way, I bought an orange drink, the whole time watching the people around me.

I arrived at Parks Manor too early for visiting hours, parked the rental car, and killed the engine. Adjusted the rearview mirror. Checked my appearance. I tucked my squeaky-clean—if frizzy—hair behind my ears, then rearranged it, unsure what to do with the unruly mess. Without hot rollers and hairspray, I felt in danger of emulating SNL's Roseanne Roseannadanna's style, but there was nothing I could do about it. Concealer covered my dark under-eye circles, but I wore the sleepless night on my face all the same.

Fierce, I stared at my reflection. "You can do this, Sandra. No reason to get upset again. Just go in and tell Iris about the note."

I inhaled, then let out a long breath and twisted my neck from side to side, psyching up for the starting gun.

One step into the lobby and my shoulders crept up toward my ears. I straightened my posture.

I'd get through this.

At least now I was sure where my mother's room was. Too bad I wasn't sure of the welcome I'd receive, especially from the girl. I grimaced. Maybe she wouldn't be there.

The double doors to my mother's wing opened, and a man walked out. Wavy hair. Familiar broad shoulders.

The last of my calm evaporated. Fear and fury collided as I looked into the face I'd seen on a daily basis. A face I'd once kissed.

Conner.

I exploded toward him, practically screaming, "What are you doing here?"

I'd flirted with the idea of Conner being some sort of lackey, but I thought I knew him. He'd never really been a contender for the role of bad guy. Not Conner. The man who held open doors and always let me voice an opinion. The man who brought me daisies on my birthday, even after we'd called off dating anymore. The man who came from a hardscrabble life and took business competition seriously.

## The Key Collector's Promise

Business. My analytical mind kicked in. Conner's betrayal made sense, in a way. He'd come here, for what? To ratchet up the threat?

Deep inside, a switch flipped, and I turned into a frightened, scorned woman.

"It was you?" I advanced on Conner, fists clenched.

Hands up, he stepped back until his spine hit the wall. "I can explain."

"Get out!" I lifted my hand to slap his face, and he caught my arm.

"Stop!"

"Let me go!" I wrenched away.

First one orderly, then another hustled over.

I pointed at Conner, my shaking finger accusing. "Grab him! He's trying to hurt my mother!"

Two of the men wrested Conner's arms behind his back.

Conner's mouth dropped open. "That's crazy! I'm not here to hurt anyone! I'd never hurt your mother!" He turned wounded eyes on me, but when that didn't work, he put on a stuffed-shirt old-man expression. He pulled himself up as much as he could while in the grip of the two muscled men. "Sandra, you're being ridiculous." Offense dripped from every word. "I can't believe you'd think it of me. Sandra…" His voice cracked.

The men let him go.

Conner seemed so sure of himself, so indignantly hurt, he almost convinced *me*.

I rallied. He had no reason to be here.

"Then why are you here? How did you find my mother's care home?"

The mental itch that had bothered me since Conner had appeared on Sycamore Street coalesced into realization, and I gasped. No one in the States knew *exactly* where I had settled, not even Addie.

I turned to the men, still standing by, watching the scene. "He's been tracing me. He followed me to England from the US and showed up yesterday at the house I recently purchased. I don't want him here."

The mood shifted once again, and the men glanced at each other. They stepped closer to Conner.

My knees wobbled, but I refused to back down. Without tearing my focus from Conner, I reached, unseeing, for the wall and steadied myself.

"That's not how it was at all!" Conner protested. "You talk about England all the time. You put pictures of properties on your bulletin board in the office, for Pete's sake."

"Oh, sure." I huffed, tamping down the quaver in my voice. "Those were general listings in England, none of which are where I ended up. I'm supposed to believe you figured out the address of exactly where I was and exactly where my mother was?"

"No." He crossed his arms. "You disappeared. I was worried, so flew over and went to your mom's last address. Asked around. June told me you'd been by and gave me the address where you were staying. When you wouldn't see me, I thought maybe if I found your mother for you, you'd talk to me. It's no big secret you've always wanted to see her again."

I was stuck back on the mention of June. "June?" I said.

June? Sweet, elderly, lonely June from my mother's old apartment complex. June, to who I'd given my phone number and told I was staying in Eden Cove.

A fiftyish man in shirtsleeves and tie approached, his shoes hitting the floor in a staccato beat. Disapproval trailed him as he called out, "Is there a problem?"

I felt like I'd gotten caught by the school principal and almost stammered out a knee-jerk denial.

The man gestured toward reception and we moved, en masse, away from the entrance to my mother's wing and back into the main area of the lobby.

All eyes turned on me.

I lifted my chin. "This man isn't supposed to be here."

"I signed in," Conner snapped.

My turn.

The grinning receptionist popped a fresh piece of gum into her mouth, clearly relishing the show.

Suspicion whirled through my mind. The break-in at number five happened after Conner arrived in England, but if he were the letter writer, why would he show up here? I'd kept my mouth shut about Strickland and was certainly out of the way.

I tossed the manager a sweet smile. "Could we go somewhere and talk things out? I'm not comfortable with this man wandering so near Iris." Shooting Conner a death glare, I leaned into the manager. "I know you value safety at this facility, and I was quite reassured before, but now?" I pointed at Conner. "I don't trust him. We need to get to the bottom of this. Why is he here?"

The man, immune to my wiles, indicated the chairs in the front waiting area. "I'll double-check he followed procedure, but he's done nothing to raise the alarm. If you need to settle your differences, feel free to talk over there."

I worried Conner would bolt, but he didn't. He strode to one of the chairs and sat as if claiming a throne. If I wanted to find out what he was up to, I had no choice but to follow.

Conner sat forward, knees apart, elbows on thighs in the classic pose men assume when they want to take up space. "Sandra, I really want to help you. What's going on? This is so unlike you."

"Maybe you don't know me as well as you think you do."

He grunted. "I know you well enough to know you aren't the kind to take off on a whim."

It was then my brain finally processed everything Conner had said since I'd caught him where he wasn't supposed to be.

June may have told him where to find me, but how had he known where to find June?

Fingers of icy dread squeezed my lungs, and I stilled, frozen and unable to draw air. For all my histrionics and anger, until now I hadn't imagined Conner capable of harming me. Not really.

I said, "Did you write the letter?"

Conner frowned. "Letter? What letter?"

I clocked no deception, no threat. But I wasn't breathing easy, either.

Before I could think better of it, I blurted out, "How did you know my mom's last address?"

The last vestiges of Conner's confidence melted. He squirmed in his seat and avoided my gaze. "I was worried, Sandy, and looked through the file cabinet. There was a copy of the file from the private eye."

A harsh bark of laughter escaped my throat. I should've been indignant, but his explanation made sense. Breaking into my files, but only for the greater good.

It was so Conner.

Either he was telling the truth or was an accomplished liar.

He ducked his head, looking at me from under his lashes. "Anything else you want to ask?"

Since he seemed willing to participate in an inquisition, I volleyed another question. "Did Daddy send you?"

Conner hunched his shoulders. Squinted at nothing. "No. Not exactly."

"What do you mean, not exactly?"

"I told him I had a personal issue to deal with. He said it was fine and to do what I needed to do. My paid time off should cover it."

*Personal issue?*

The man had dated me, then lost interest and relegated me to nothing but friendly co-worker status, not the sort of relationship to justify chasing me across the globe.

He was up to no good. Him coming to England made no sense.

Unless he really had come for me.

My heart did a slow flip. For a second, I let a rose-colored haze blind me, but then dismissed the idea. If he'd wanted me, he would've acted on it before now.

I said, "Why would you tell him that?"

He frowned. "What do you mean, why?" The frown turned into a scowl worthy of the grumpy old men on the Muppet show. "I just told you. You ran off. You're acting weird." He crossed his arms and jutted out his chin.

I should've held my tongue, but fear-driven adrenalin made my defenses trigger-happy, and Conner Harrison had a way of rattling me.

I snapped back, "Well, you tell me who's acting weird. Stalking me to England, showing up at my home out of nowhere, and then having the unmitigated gall to visit my mother, let's not mention breaking into my house."

Conner straightened. He stared, round-eyed in alarm, a narrow rim of topaz showing around his dilated pupils. He grabbed my wrist. "Who broke in? Where? When?"

I lost all my words.

When I didn't respond, he shook me by the arm. "Sandra! Tell me what's going on right now or I *will* call your father, I swear it."

## Chapter Twenty-Two

*June 1, WEDNESDAY Cont.*

"Sandra?"

A tremulous voice snatched my attention, and I spun around. Iris, sitting in a wheelchair, gaped at me as if she'd seen a ghost.

All I could squeeze out was a single syllable. "Mum?"

"I thought I'd dreamed you."

"No. I'm here. I came."

We stared at each other—I'm not sure for how long—before I noticed the young woman behind her. The girl, the same brunette I'd seen in Mum's room. She stood, statue-still, gripping the wheelchair handles.

Conner's breath tickled my ear. "Let's find somewhere for you two to talk."

When had he come to stand beside me? I should've stepped away but, oddly, couldn't bear to leave his side.

"Yes," I said, my voice little-girl quiet.

"The garden is empty." Conner's gaze flicked to my mum. My *mum*. He spoke to her. "Or would you rather Sandra came to your room?"

The brunette piped up. "No. The garden is fine." Her nostrils flared. "I know you."

She knew me? Had Iris told her about me?

"You came yesterday." Hackles up, she looked ready to spit. "You didn't say…" She clamped her mouth shut. Placing a hand on my mum's shoulder, she bent close, but l heard her plain when she asked, "Do you want to go into the garden and talk with them? You don't have to, you know."

A stunned Mum reached back and absently patted the girl's hand. "Out in the garden, please, Christine. That's a good girl."

The young woman, Christine, looked me up-and-down in a perfect mean girl imitation.

I kept my face blank as she and Iris led the way.

Conner muttered, "Christine sure reminds me of you."

I stumbled and he caught me, but by then I'd gathered my senses and jerked away. Christine and I were nothing alike. The girl dressed like a teen in her too-tight, red and white striped T-shirt and equally as tight jeans.

The fresh air of the garden brought me a notch toward regaining composure. Mum appeared dazed. The rest of us stood around, waiting for something. Me, I supposed.

I asked Christine, "Is she on pain meds today?"

Christine tossed her head and scoffed. "She just had her foot lopped off. What do you think?"

My jaw hit the ground. "What?"

"My foot wasn't lopped off, Christine," Mum admonished. "No need to be that way."

The reprimand had the air of a well-worn shtick. Christine didn't react to Iris. Instead, she glowered at me.

I noted the boot on Iris's right foot. "What happened?"

Blushing, Mum folded her hands in her lap. "I had a toe removed."

"A toe?" I gasped. "What happened?"

"A complication of diabetes. It was weeks ago. I'm nearly better. It was only one, my pinkie."

Only one? How many toes did it take for it to be a big deal?

Iris dipped her head, almost as if she were ashamed. The topic clearly made her uncomfortable.

Time to change the subject, get on with my mission. "I hate to hear you're feeling poorly, and I'd come back later, but…"

She glanced up, her face paling. "Please don't leave just yet."

"All right." With a calming gesture, I patted the air with my hands, and then indicated a pair of stone benches. "Let's sit."

Color returned to Mum's cheeks, pinking them slightly. All her earlier confusion had gone. "Yes. Let's do." As if taken by a chill, she wrapped her knitted cardigan about her tighter.

Christine wheeled her over to one bench and sat, but Conner hung back.

He said, "Should I wait for you in the lobby?"

Too much was happening, too fast, not the least of which was a strange desire to keep him by my side. Conner, who a scant ten minutes ago had rocketed to the top of my suspect list, before he'd had me second-guessing myself again. I hesitated, torn between following him and demanding explanations, or staying with Iris.

My indecision must've been easy to gauge, because he said, "I'll wait for you."

Warning Iris had precedence, didn't it? And somehow the set of Conner's jaw made me believe he'd wait. The minute I nodded, he left the garden.

I perched on the second stone bench, crossed and uncrossed my ankles. I cleared my throat. All the ways of approaching the topic of the letter had flown from my mind.

I said, "How are you?"

Lame.

Mum gave me a watery smile. "It's lovely to see you." Her face crumpled, and she began to cry in earnest.

I had no idea what to do and sat like a lump. Should I offer water? Go find an attendant?

Christine knelt at my mum's feet, heedless of what the concrete pathway would do to her jeans. "Don't go on so. It's all right." She patted Mum's knee.

Mum dug a tissue from her cardigan pocket and waved Christine's concern away. "Don't mind me. It's the shock."

I swallowed hard. "I'm sorry."

"Don't be. I'm glad you came to find me. I was never certain if I should try to contact you once you'd grown. And before…" she trailed off. "None of that matters. You're here now."

"Yes." I'd better get it out. "I came to tell you about a letter I received." My chest tightened, but I got enough air to say, "I have to warn you."

As I told the story of the letter, the meeting with Strickland, my worry Daddy had gotten in over his head, and my trip to England, Christine's posture shifted from glowering hostility to disbelief to caution. "Are you sure this Strickland character could do harm from the US?"

"I hope not." Acutely aware of Mum slumping into her wheelchair, I picked my next words carefully. "But the man is powerful. He scares me," I admitted. "And I've had a break-in, which probably isn't related."

Afraid of being labeled an alarmist, I decided against mentioning the second note, for now. I couldn't prove the same person had written it. And citing my vague, intermittent feelings of being watched wouldn't advance my cause with Christine, either.

I finished up with, "I have concerns. I'd like to make sure the security here is aware and can keep you safe. Doubtless once the deal goes through, there won't be any threat."

Mum rubbed her forehead. "I don't know what to make of all this."

"Understandable." I'd barely had time to process the situation myself.

Christine blurted out. "What about notifying the police?"

"No!"

Both women startled, though my mum recovered first.

"I don't want my father to get caught up in an investigation."

Iris gave a slow nod, as if she understood me perfectly.

Christine said, "That's ridiculous. If he has done nothing wrong, he shouldn't worry about an investigation."

The only problem was, I didn't know if Daddy was completely innocent of wrongdoing. He'd been willing to go in with Strickland. Had he been willing to do more? The dark thought haunting me finally came into the light. Had Daddy written the note?

How many times over the years had he insisted, "It's for your own good."

I flashed to long, lonely days at subpar summer camps, brutal sports sessions, and harsh school tutors. Daddy's methods were all the harder to take because of their calculated nature and his absolute belief he was doing the right thing, even when he wasn't.

This was not a revelation I wanted to share with Christine.

I said, "Look. It's important the warning is taken seriously." I turned to my mum. "You understand, don't you? I don't want to involve Daddy."

She scanned my face as if she could read me. Then she nodded. "All right."

"I'll go request an audience with the care home director and we'll let him know about the threat."

# Chapter Twenty-Three

*June 1, WEDNESDAY Cont.*

I poked my head into the lobby, relieved to see Conner hadn't run off. After I explained to him about meeting with the care home director about security, he insisted on accompanying us down the hall, and waited outside with an attendant, who eyed him with more curiosity than suspicion.

Conner leaned against the wall, relaxed and arms folded across his chest, as if he could wait all day.

Mum, Christine, and I squeezed into the director's small office. The man sat behind a plain desk. A large blotter covered most of its surface, leaving a corner for his speakerphone. Two hard plastic chairs faced the desk. I sat in one and Christine took the other, with Mum in her wheelchair on Christine's other side. After he'd reassured us, I spoke up.

"And you can affirm there will be extra security measures?"

"Oh, yes. Our staff boasts a retired constable. We've never had a hint of trouble." He ran a hand over his low side-part and across his balding dome. "If any suspicious characters turn up, be assured we'll ring you immediately. I assume you'll do the same." He shot me a stern warning look, the first indication he considered the threat more than my wild imagination. Should I be glad he'd taken it seriously, or concerned he might boot Mum out for needing extra attention?

With perfect posture, I treated him to my best sales smile. "Of course!" Slathering a hint of honey butter on top of a southern drawl, I said, "For certain we can count on you to take good care of her."

I could tell Christine wanted to roll her eyes, but she maintained her bored demeanor, picking imaginary lint from her jeans.

The director beamed. "That we will."

Christine hopped up. "Thank you, Mr. Williams." She gripped the handles of Mum's wheelchair and maneuvered it around.

Scrambling to my feet, I nodded at the director. "Thank you."

Outside the office, Conner had remained in the same position, but came alongside me as I hurried after Christine, my eyes glued to her back. The girl set my teeth on edge, and it was hard to muster the pity I should feel for upending her life. The shock of a long-lost sister appearing had to be equal parts upsetting and confusing.

I should know.

Was Christine my biological sister? Or just someone who'd filled the role that should've been mine?

My chin wobbled. I swallowed hard.

Conner's hand found the small of my back. I hazarded a quick glance his way, but his gaze stayed fixed straight ahead. Good. The last thing I wanted was sympathy. I wanted a strong arm to lean on and someone to have my back. In the past,

## The Key Collector's Promise

Conner had been that. Except when it came to a choice between me and Daddy. But then, he was here with me now, wasn't he?

For the rest of the awkward visit, Christine never left my mother's side, though Conner ducked out, saying he'd be in the lobby. This time I had no doubt he'd be there when I finished my visit.

When Mum said she was tired, I took the hint, pasted on a smile, and made as if to leave.

Mum reached for me. "Leave your number." She dropped her hand. "If you don't mind."

Sweetness filled me, light as cotton candy. She wanted my number.

It was hard not to wish for more.

"Of course I'll give you my number."

"I'll ring you. I want to see you again."

"Call anytime." I scribbled my Eden Cove phone number and address on a notepad by her bed and showed it to her.

"That's nice. Suffolk by the sea."

I wanted to ask if she remembered the sycamore tree at the summer cottage, but tucked the question away for another day. Cracking open memories could wait.

Christine got up. "I'll walk you out."

The muscles in my neck bunched. I had the urge to shake out my arms like a boxer about to head into the ring.

We walked out together, not speaking, me in front, and were almost to the double doors when Christine said, "Hang on."

Here it came.

I pivoted, my face as bland and emotionless as I could manage. I'd expected hostility, but the scowl I'd come to think of as Christine's permanent expression had fled. She reminded me of a scared twelve-year-old. I knew what that felt like. My softening must've shown, because she lifted her chin, defiant.

"I'm not sold on this idea of a threat. How do I know you're not just making it up?"

Beneath her bravado, fear sparked in her eyes. I couldn't blame her for her suspicions. If the tables were turned, I'd feel the same. "I get you don't know me and have no reason to believe me, but it wasn't my aim to upset Iris. I only want to keep her safe."

Christine worked her jaw. I could almost hear the wheels in her mind spinning.

Finally, she crossed her arms and demanded, "What exactly did the letter say?"

I didn't want to think about it, much less say it, but swallowed the bile rising in my throat and recited, "What is your heart's desire? True love, a vacation on an island, a safe place to lay your head at night? Girls who talk too much lose precious things. Keep your mouth shut about the Strickland Project. Remember, family first."

Christine pointed out. "Then the letter doesn't mention my mum specifically. You barely know her. Do you have family in the US?"

"Just my father."

*My father.*

My vision tunneled and grew dim as every bit of air deflated from my lungs.

I stared at Christine. "I hadn't thought of that."

Could the letter be referring to Daddy? I shook my head, almost told her that made no sense. I'd been operating on intuition, or so I'd told myself, but why couldn't it be Daddy?

Because why would anyone threaten him? He was needed for the Strickland deal. Wasn't he? Doubt traced my spine like an ice-cold finger. None of which I could explain to this angry girl in the hall of my mother's care home.

I said, "I just want Iris to be safe."

Christine crossed her arms and gave a grudging nod. "Okay."

---

Conner sat in the lobby, one foot propped on the opposite knee.

At least *he* was relaxed.

He stood and assessed me, but not in a confrontational way. More like approaching skittish wildlife. "You still want to hash it out here?"

I sensed no threat from him. Quite the opposite. The temptation to curl into him swamped me.

I blurted out, "Conner, can I trust you?"

His response was immediate, with not a speck of righteous indignation this time. "I'd never do anything to hurt you, Sandra. Never. Tell me you know that."

My temples throbbed and I pressed my fingers to my head. "I don't know anything anymore."

He shifted on his feet, sliding his hands into his back pockets. "Sandra, I'm sorry. Frightening you wasn't my intention. I tracked you down because, well…" His brow puckered and he made an awful face, like he'd taken a bite of a bitter persimmon. "*I* was scared. For you. Worried."

The admission cost him, and I found the fact ridiculously attractive. He looked so earnest. I could get lost in those eyes.

He said, "A couple of your clients called looking for you. And Addie seems upset. The office feels strange without you there."

The office. Work.

The heat warming my core cooled. With Conner, didn't it always come back to work? It was a reminder, though, to keep my head on straight.

He said, "Why are you here? And why does your mother need extra security?"

When I'd seen him, I'd been the one full of questions, and I still was. What did he know about Strickland? What had he and Daddy been doing on that trip out of town, or other meetings I hadn't been privy to?

And how much should I tell him.

I picked over the landmine of words crowding my head. "I'm worried about Daddy. You know I don't want him in partnership with Strickland." I licked my lips. "Do you know anything about a letter left for me at the office?"

He frowned and raked his hand through his hair. "What kind of letter? You'll have to be more specific."

"If I tell you, you have to promise to keep it in confidence."

"This isn't making me feel any better, Sandy."

"Promise."

He pinned me with a serious look. "All right. I'll keep your secret."

"I got a letter at the office warning me off any interference with the Strickland deal. A letter that sent me here to check on my mother."

He jerked upright, and his face drained of color. "Did you tell your father?"

I closed my eyes. "No. And I'm not going to. Neither are you."

"But why?"

"Because I don't know what Daddy has gotten into, or how deep."

I crossed my arms, a protective move. I had to bite my tongue to keep from demanding he tell me what he knew about Daddy's dealings. Instead, I waited for him to volunteer. The silence stretched, and Conner's expression shifted from choir-boy innocent confusion to shock, and then his face went blank. Without being asked a direct question, he'd remain a passive as polished granite.

A mirror to his neutral stance, I stripped all emotion from my thoughts and asked, "Did you write the letter?"

"No."

No hesitation, no guile in the answer. It was something, at least. I'd never known Conner to lie.

I let out a breath. "It's getting late."

I wanted to tell him to stay away from my mum. Just as badly, I wanted to trust him and confide all, including my new worries about Daddy being a possible target. The sweet old lady, June, might've done me a favor by telling Conner where to find me. My heart told me I could trust him, but I couldn't bring myself to take him into confidence completely. Not yet. Not when it involved a real estate deal or Daddy's business decisions.

Earnest lines bracketed his mouth, and his eyes were as dark as a midnight storm. He reached for me and held onto my forearm, his grasp firm, yet gentle. "Sandy, you worried about your mother having security. What about for you?"

"I'll be careful."

When I pulled away, he let go of me physically, but his intense scrutiny help be captive like a butterfly in a jar.

I needed space from him before I spilled out the whole story, so I got up, mumbled a goodbye, and walked away.

On my way back to Sycamore Street, I stopped at a Dixons electronics store and bought an answering machine for the telephone. If Iris called, I didn't want to miss it.

When I came out of Dixons, I found Conner leaning against my car, one long, lean, denim-clad leg across the other. He wore his broke-in cowboy boots. The sight of him made me homesick for easy nights watching movies and sharing popcorn, afternoon boat rides, and sweet tea on the patio. I'd missed the familiar comforts of home—and Conner.

The truth startled me, and I tamped down on my wayward emotions.

Homesickness. That's all it was. A case of homesickness.

"What are you doing?" My tone was cool but had no bite.

"Waiting for you."

Enigmatic as always.

"I don't need you to look after me."

"That's what you said."

The parking lot of an electronic store in the middle of a strange town wasn't my best choice for a showdown. Besides, he wasn't hurting anything.

I scooched around him, and he moved so I could get in. I drove away. As I glanced in the rearview, I saw him, his posture relaxed, watching me leave.

# Chapter Twenty-Four

*June 1, WEDNESDAY Cont.*

The drive to Eden Cove gave me time to rehash and sort my many worries, and I settled on Daddy to obsess over. Logic dictated there was no need for concern. Even so, once awakened, the fear he might be in danger nibbled at me. I'd phone Daddy and put it to rest. Besides, I'd been avoiding the call long enough.

At the house, Oscar greeted me with a wagging tail and a happy grin.

I squatted and gave him a good scratch behind the ears. "At least I know where I stand with you, Oscar."

He pressed a wet nose into my palm, snuffling. Finding my hand empty, his focus swung from me to the kitchen and back again.

"I see how it is. You're happy to see me as long as I feed you. All right. I'll get your supper."

After pouring kibble into the dog's bowl and refilling his water, I hooked up the answering machine while attempting to work out what I should say to Daddy.

The first stars of evening had peeped out over the Deben River, but with the time difference, it was barely lunchtime in Louisiana.

I picked up the phone and dialed the office.

Addie answered in her usual cheery tone.

"Oh, Addie," I said. "It's so good to hear your voice."

"Are you all right?" The worry came through so clearly I pictured her forehead wrinkling.

As far as Addie knew, I was on a simple trip. I had to stop acting weird.

Self-conscious, I laughed. "I'm fine. Just missed you. You'd love the countryside here. There are flowers everywhere, views of the sea, and even nearby castle ruins. It's very picturesque."

Addie breathed a chuckle. "The place sounds nice. You scared me there for a moment."

"Sorry." I twisted the phone cord. "Is Daddy in?"

"I'm sorry, hon. He's not. Should I tell him you called?"

It wasn't unusual for Daddy to be out of the office, but it frustrated me. I wanted to speak with him.

"Is he well?"

"Of course! Why do you ask? Sandra, what's going on?"

*Way to go, Sandra.*

The last thing I wanted was to upset Addie. I pinched the bridge of my nose and dove in. "I just wanted to check on him. Make sure all the upcoming projects are as they should be."

"You're still fretting about Strickland, aren't you?"

So much for subtlety.

"Actually, yes."

"I'll tell him. But don't worry, hon." Her tone had an edge. "Your father knows what he's doing. I think you should let him handle it while you enjoy your trip."

She said it with such an odd coldness I took the receiver away from my ear and stared at it in surprise.

After a beat, I put the phone back to my ear. "If you could just let him know I called."

"Will do." She sounded her normal self. Happy, even. Had I read too much into our exchange?

After I hung up, I kicked myself for leaving a message. If I called again too soon, Daddy would think it strange. I'd give it a day. But if I knew Addie, she'd relay the message. In fact, my concern might come better from her than me.

At least it was done, and I felt better for having it off my list. I went into the kitchen and made myself a turkey sandwich. I'd just taken a huge bite when someone knocked at the door.

Conner stood across my threshold, his brown eyes dark in the gathering twilight. Relaxed, no smile, throwing off protective energy, controlled but as dangerous as a big cat. I'd never seen him act this way before.

I shivered, glad he was on my side.

He said, "You're not staying here with no one watching out for you. I can sleep in my car, but let your friend down the way know. Otherwise, she'll call the police on me, I'm sure." With a chin lift, he gestured towards Harriet's door. "Better yet, go stay with her. I'd like to explain things to her, but thought you might prefer to do it yourself."

Did he think because he'd gone all Conan the Barbarian he could boss me around?

"Conner," I said, but then had nothing else of substance to add.

Stubborn, infuriating man. And he would stick to his word.

I opened the door wide. "Oh, come in."

He grinned, and bodyguard Conner disappeared, replaced by the sweet guy who'd brought me a teddy bear for Valentine's Day once upon a time. "Thought you'd never ask."

Conner entered the house, and Oscar bounded over, his propeller tail going full speed. Kneeling on one knee, Conner rubbed the dog's neck and head. "Hey-ya, champ. Been looking after Sandy? That's your job."

So now he was giving my dog assignments?

*The* dog, I corrected myself. Just because I'd adopted the name Kenny chose didn't mean the dog belonged to me.

Conner squinted up at me. "Will you let me back in if I go to my car for my stuff?"

I crossed my arms. "Of course."

"I want to call Whit, tell him what's going on. If you're in danger, he should know."

"That's not your place, Conner. I'd prefer you stay out of my relationship with Daddy."

He pursed his lips tight enough to turn them pale.

I went on. "If you must know, I already called the office and left a message."

It wasn't even a lie.

---

The next day, Conner replaced the fidgety handle on the upstairs toilet, stripped the wallpaper in the living room, and then set to patching holes in the drywall.

I let him. He was almost as good a handyman as he thought he was, and I wasn't about to stop him. What else would we do while I waited for Iris to call or Strickland's goons to break another window? Talk?

## The Key Collector's Promise

Hastily, I cracked open a can of spackle and set to work filling a nail hole. A boom box sat near the fireplace, and Conner had popped in a mix tape he'd recorded.

"Don't Mess with My Toot, Toot" began playing, and my hips wiggled all on their own. Before I knew it, Conner was dancing me around the living room to Zydeco. At the lyrics about the baby, we separated and gave the usual loud single handclap along with the song.

He spun me once, twice, three times. I lost my footing, but he kept a tight grip, and I ended up crushed against his chest, laughing.

So close the heat of his breath warmed my ear, he said, "I should take you dancing when we get back home."

Home. And get dumped again?

I stiffened, and he immediately loosened his hold but didn't let go until I stepped back.

I said, "We better finish up in here."

Conner ran a hand over the top of his head, attempting to tame his wild locks but they only sprang out more. I squelched the urge to let my fingers untangle his dark, black-brown waves.

Conner picked up a rag. "I guess you're right."

The song changed to "Under Pressure."

A song matching my mood exactly.

## Chapter Twenty-Five

*June 3, FRIDAY Late Morning*

"Look at this old book I found." More animated than he'd been since we'd stopped dancing and set to work the day before, Conner bounded down the stairs two at a time and held out a fabric-bound copy. "It was in the back of the closet."

He'd been working upstairs as I sanded the stair rail, readying it for a coat of paint.

We stood next to each other, him leafing through the pages of a very old copy of *The Last of the Mohicans*. I hadn't known how old the story was. A card fluttered to the stair tread and I picked it up.

Yellowed with age, it bore old-fashioned spidery handwriting inside.

*Happy Fourteenth Birthday Charles,*

*I know how you love your stories and thought you might enjoy this one. It's one from Mr. Bookman's collection, and I know you will take good care of it.*

*Love,*
*Grandmother*

## The Key Collector's Promise

"Read this." I passed the note to Conner, trading it for the book. It had a few splotches of indeterminate origin and a few loose pages, but no dog-eared edges. I smiled at Conner, glad his discovery had broken the tense silence that had pervaded the house.

I said, "I wonder what other treasures you might find in this old place." The comment had been random, and I hadn't meant anything by it, but somehow the air grew thick with meaning. I'd pushed him away earlier, but wasn't sure I could again.

"Sandra…"

The shrill ring of the phone pierced the air, breaking the moment.

I passed him the book. "I better get the phone."

On my way down, my sock-clad feet barely kept traction on the stair treads. In the middle of the third ring, I picked up before the answering machine could click on. "Hello?"

"Sandra? It's me."

My heart squeezed at her voice. Mum.

"Yes?" I said. "Is everything all right?"

"Right as rain."

Hardly likely, but I took her response to mean nothing terrible had happened.

She said, "I wanted to see you soon, if you could manage."

"Of course." I checked my watch and did a quick calculation. "I can come at two."

"Christine has to work this afternoon."

"Ah," I said, not sure how to respond.

"See you then." Mum clicked off.

Mum wanted to talk with me without Christine around. Was it bad to feel a smidge of satisfaction? Maybe not. It depended on why Iris wanted to meet alone with me.

I headed upstairs to hunt for shoes. Sawdust frosted my jeans and T-shirt, adding to the speckles of paint. I should change, but I was fast running through my wardrobe. Business attire didn't feel right for this visit. Too stiff and formal.

I brushed at my jeans. At the very least, I had to swap out the T-shirt for my white button-up.

If it wasn't too wrinkled.

Conner stood at the top of the stairs. "You look pensive. What's going on?"

I told him, and he insisted on driving me. For once I didn't fight him. I had the shakes, more nervous now than the first time I visited.

We got to Parks Manor, and Conner walked me down the hall to Iris's room, letting one hand smooth down my back.

"Are you going to be okay?"

"I'll be fine." I wasn't at all sure I'd be fine. My fingers skimmed Conner's forearm, lingering on his warm skin. For no reason at all, I noticed he smelled of cinnamon and warm bread.

Mum sat in her room in a brown plaid upholstered chair, cup of tea in hand, with a pair of crutches nearby. A matching chair to the left of hers barely fit in the space. I didn't remember seeing them in her room before, but I'd been distracted.

She set her tea down on a small side table. "I'm so glad you came!" Clasping her hands in her lap, she offered a tremulous, close-lipped smile.

Her display of nerves calmed my own, and I spoke softly. "I'm glad you called. You're doing better?"

"Read this." I passed the note to Conner, trading it for the book. It had a few splotches of indeterminate origin and a few loose pages, but no dog-eared edges. I smiled at Conner, glad his discovery had broken the tense silence that had pervaded the house.

I said, "I wonder what other treasures you might find in this old place." The comment had been random, and I hadn't meant anything by it, but somehow the air grew thick with meaning. I'd pushed him away earlier, but wasn't sure I could again.

"Sandra..."

The shrill ring of the phone pierced the air, breaking the moment.

I passed him the book. "I better get the phone."

On my way down, my sock-clad feet barely kept traction on the stair treads. In the middle of the third ring, I picked up before the answering machine could click on. "Hello?"

"Sandra? It's me."

My heart squeezed at her voice. Mum.

"Yes?" I said. "Is everything all right?"

"Right as rain."

Hardly likely, but I took her response to mean nothing terrible had happened.

She said, "I wanted to see you soon, if you could manage."

"Of course." I checked my watch and did a quick calculation. "I can come at two."

"Christine has to work this afternoon."

"Ah," I said, not sure how to respond.

"See you then." Mum clicked off.

Mum wanted to talk with me without Christine around. Was it bad to feel a smidge of satisfaction? Maybe not. It depended on why Iris wanted to meet alone with me.

I headed upstairs to hunt for shoes. Sawdust frosted my jeans and T-shirt, adding to the speckles of paint. I should change, but I was fast running through my wardrobe. Business attire didn't feel right for this visit. Too stiff and formal.

I brushed at my jeans. At the very least, I had to swap out the T-shirt for my white button-up.

If it wasn't too wrinkled.

Conner stood at the top of the stairs. "You look pensive. What's going on?"

I told him, and he insisted on driving me. For once I didn't fight him. I had the shakes, more nervous now than the first time I visited.

We got to Parks Manor, and Conner walked me down the hall to Iris's room, letting one hand smooth down my back.

"Are you going to be okay?"

"I'll be fine." I wasn't at all sure I'd be fine. My fingers skimmed Conner's forearm, lingering on his warm skin. For no reason at all, I noticed he smelled of cinnamon and warm bread.

Mum sat in her room in a brown plaid upholstered chair, cup of tea in hand, with a pair of crutches nearby. A matching chair to the left of hers barely fit in the space. I didn't remember seeing them in her room before, but I'd been distracted.

She set her tea down on a small side table. "I'm so glad you came!" Clasping her hands in her lap, she offered a tremulous, close-lipped smile.

Her display of nerves calmed my own, and I spoke softly. "I'm glad you called. You're doing better?"

## The Key Collector's Promise

"Oh, yes. The surgery was ages ago. I still use the wheelchair a bit, but I enjoy getting around without it when I can." She patted the chair beside her. "Sit." Furrowing her brow apologetically at Conner, she said, "Sorry there's not another seat for you. I can ask for an extra chair."

Conner lifted his hands. "No need. Just stopping in to say hi. I have a tape I want to listen to." He patted his jacket pocket and showed her a Walkman.

Turning, he winked at me.

The middle of my chest felt achy and too full, a pleasant pain I hadn't experienced before. It put me in mind of sweet molasses, but when the door whispered shut behind him, the feeling went with him, and I was left with no one to lean on except myself.

I perched on the seat beside Iris, acutely aware of my body, all stiff joints and uncertain angles. Balancing my purse awkwardly on my knees, I forced a lilt into my voice, "What should we talk about?"

"I need to explain about Christine."

I should've been ready, but I flinched as if I'd been slapped.

Was this the part where she told me why she kept Christine, but let me go? I brought my purse tight against my belly, wishing I hadn't come.

"Christine is your cousin."

"My cousin?" I echoed, struggling to place Christine into a different slot on the family tree.

Iris rubbed her forehead. "My sister's child. Christine was only a baby when she died."

"Oh." I deflated back into the chair. I had an aunt. Who had died. "I'm so sorry."

It explained Christine's presence, and maybe why she called Iris her mum.

No relief came. It didn't answer the question that had haunted me my entire childhood. Why hadn't my mother looked for me? An image of Daddy when he'd been crossed flashed in my mind, unyielding posture and flinty eyes. Did I want to know if she'd tried and he'd stopped her?

"You still have it!" Iris extended a trembling hand, then withdrew it, but her eyes remained fixed on my chest.

The hard ridges of the key bit into my palm. Without knowing it, I'd been handling the key on its chain.

"I promised."

Iris's chin quivered. "I wish things could've been different."

The tick-tock of the wall clock went along its merry way as accusations and entreaties for reconciliation stuck in my throat. I coughed. Swallowed.

"So do I."

All Daddy had done for me leapt to mind. While not always perfect, at least he'd been a constant presence in my life—a stark contrast to the black hole of my mother's absence.

I added, "Sometimes I wanted a different life, but Daddy was good to me." Rigid in my chair, I waited for her to say a negative comment about Daddy, but she didn't.

Instead, she seemed to mull it over. I unbent the slightest bit. This woman was careful with her words, something I understood and respected.

She opened the small drawer of the side table and retrieved a battered box of drugstore greeting cards, only when she opened the box, it didn't hold cards. It was full of folded scraps of paper and memorabilia. A beaded bracelet, photos, and a tiny envelope, the adhesive on its flap useless and discolored. One by one, she took out items and gave them to me.

I frowned at a childish drawing and read the wobbly drawn name in blue crayon. Sandra.

My breath caught.

The stick figures with giant heads holding hands were Mum and me.

These were my belongings.

I fingered the child's bracelet, hoping for a memory. None came. To me, it was only a string of old plastic beads.

She reclaimed the small envelope and opened it with shaky fingers. "This is a lock of hair from your first haircut."

Blonde. Yellow-blonde, like hers.

My hair color had changed by the time I turned six. In every school photo, it was dark brown, like Daddy's. I had no memory of this pale blonde color ever belonging to me.

She said, "It should be in your baby book, I know, but I like to keep it here. I have lots of pictures, too."

I should've been touched. It was a sweet gesture, but these memories were hers, not mine. They left me empty. I wanted to dredge up the old hurt. I'd told myself a hundred times she could've stood up to Daddy. Beside her now, I wasn't so sure, and not simply because of her health. If she'd ever had a fighting spirit, it had turned as frail as her body.

Flushed and overeager, she said, "Would you like to see your baby book? Or my other photo albums? They're in the cabinet just over there."

As much as I wanted to connect with Iris, I couldn't bear to wade through her memories of baby Sandra, photos of a child I didn't recognize. "I can't right now." Forced by my southern manners, an upbringing she had no part in, I reminded myself, I murmured a polite, "Another time."

"Well, that's all right, then." She lowered her lashes and studied the empty box in her lap.

Carefully, I refolded the drawing and placed the things back into the box. Just as carefully, Iris replaced the lid.

I said, "Why didn't you keep in touch?"

"I'd made terrible mistakes. You have to understand, I was so young." Iris sat rigid, holding the box on her knees. "I loved you. I always loved you. You have to believe me." The plea was desperate.

*You have to believe me.*

Why did I have to believe her? I swallowed down a sour reply demanding proof. Reforming habits bred by hurt take a long time. I wasn't ready to open myself to this stranger who was my mother.

Her fingers picked at the box. "I was afraid you wouldn't want me around. Afraid of ruining your life. And I had other fears."

My lungs seized. Was she going to tell me about Daddy? I waited, aching to hear while at the same time fighting the urge to get up and flee. It took all my concentration to remain seated.

She carried on.

"Oh Sandra, I'd made a mess of my marriage. I treated your father badly, and worse, I wasn't the best mother."

Daddy had told me she'd cheated on him. She was untrustworthy. I waited for more details, her side of the story, a dark secret to explain the biggest whys in my life.

"What happened?"

## The Key Collector's Promise

Avoiding my eyes, Iris rubbed the top of her thighs. "We were so young, and we fought all the time, over everything—money, friends, silly things like what kind of bread to buy." She dabbed at her upper lip. "I fell in love with someone else." Clasping her hands, she gave me a beseeching look. "I didn't mean to. Your dad and I had a huge fight, and I took you away to the cottage without telling him where we were going. That was wrong. If I could go back and change it, I would." As if realizing she'd said more than she'd meant to, she shut her mouth.

I'd known, or at least suspected, the story she told, minus the part about her taking me away. That wouldn't have set well with Daddy.

I said, "Were you afraid of my father?"

"Married people fight." Her face closed up. The silence stretched out. Finally, she said, "I was hoping we could get to know each other. You'll come back?" Hands shaking, she lifted the box to put it on the side table.

Her chest rose and fell.

There would be no more answers today. The muscles in my neck unknotted, leaving behind fatigue and soreness I would feel the next day.

I said, "I think getting to know each other is a good place to start."

Over the next few days, I visited Iris in the afternoons. If I tried to wheedle stories about Daddy out of her or touch on their relationship, she clammed up. Conflict of any sort set her on edge. She went into palpitations during an argument with another resident over Prime Minister Margaret Thatcher.

I learned to avoid heavy topics and instead concentrated on getting to know Mum and winning Christine over, and by Sunday, Christine had started to loosen up a little.

Security at Parks Manor seemed up to snuff.

No more odd events happened on Sycamore Street. Just the same, Conner shadowed me everywhere. There was no more dancing in the living room, but he steadily whittled away at the house repair list, and I stopped asking him how long he planned to stay in England.

## Chapter Twenty-Six

*June 6, MONDAY Afternoon*

Iris smiled and reclaimed her cup of tea, stone cold by now. "Would you like a cuppa? I can ask for the attendant to bring one."

"No, thank you."

She put her cup back down. "I wondered," she plucked at the hem of her floral blouse. "Perhaps we could go for a drive?"

"A drive?" I frowned at her foot with its medical boot. "Will they let me take you out?"

She laughed. An almost-memory swamped me, iridescent and fleeting, a hint of warm milk and soft arms. The longing nearly undid me.

She said, "It's not a prison."

I blinked. "What?"

"It feels like one sometimes, but they can't keep me in."

"But what about the security? We can't take the guard with us, and it's not safe to go out without one."

"I'm not afraid, Sandra. I caved in to fear and made a terrible mistake, letting you go. Look what it cost us." She retrieved a tissue from her pocket and dabbed her eyes. "Would you like to go by the old summer rental cottage? Since you kept the key all this time, I thought you might want to see it again, though I haven't a clue who owns it now. We wouldn't be able to go in, of course."

The old cottage. I touched the key at my neck.

I must've looked as uncertain as I felt, because she said, "Don't worry so. Your young man can look out for us."

*My young man?*

"Conner's not…"

What was Conner, exactly?

"We wouldn't have to visit the old cottage, if you'd rather not. Just a drive out would be fun. You don't think he'd go for it?"

"No, I mean, yes. I mean…" I floundered before finally hitting on an answer. "Let's talk to security and see what they say."

With the extra safety measures we'd requested and the warnings I'd given, surely the staff wouldn't be keen on letting her go off with me and Conner. After all, we were strangers.

My assessment turned out to be wrong. The nurse gushed about how wonderful an outing would be, and likely to help Iris's recovery along, and other staff members agreed. Thrilled as a child on the way to a school carnival, Iris glowed with happiness. How could I throw cold water on her plan to drive to the cottage? A car ride was such a small thing.

With the help of her crutches, Iris headed for the hall.

"We're bringing the wheelchair," I said, concern making me gruff. "We might need it."

She only nodded and kept on her way. Once we got to the lobby, Conner joined our little expedition.

Iris beamed at him. "The nurse said an outing is the perfect thing for me, and Sandra's taking me out."

"Is that so?" Conner's eyebrows climbed up his forehead and he shot me a skeptical look.

"The staff okayed it." I shrugged, unwilling to ruin Iris's happiness and trying to convince myself everything would be fine.

With me manning the empty wheelchair, we slowly made our way out to the car, Conner and Iris chatting like old friends, discussing a television show I'd never heard of.

After he settled Iris into the front passenger seat, he came around to the rear of the car where I was attempting to wrestle the chair into the trunk.

"Here. Let me." He hefted it with ease and stowed the thing away.

"I would have gotten it." This idea of a trip made me uneasy, not enough to back out, though. I'd keep a watchful eye out.

As had become our custom, Conner got into the driver's seat. Iris beamed at me from my usual spot beside him.

It would be fine. I'd be vigilant for anyone following, and Conner was no slouch. He said something about the show, and the two of them picked up their conversation while I slid into the backseat, the place for small children and third wheels.

Iris called to me, "Do you watch British comedies?"

"Not really," I said.

As we motored away, Conner met my eye in the rear view. "Aren't you glad I came along?"

I was, but felt off-balance, and irritated at him for no good reason, finding it impossible to stop huffing. Then it hit me.

I wasn't irritated. I was jealous.

Was this why siblings fought for their mother's attention? Scraping up my dignity, I readjusted, blowing my hair from my face, as if the unmanageable locks were the reason for my huffing and puffing.

I touched the seatback near Iris. "Are you sure you know the way?"

"Oh, yes."

Belatedly, I answered Conner's earlier question, leaning close to his ear. "I *am* glad you're here."

He gave a slow wink, coupled with an almost sad knowing. Irritation prodded me again, ruffling my feathers. I wanted to tell him to stop feeling sorry for me, but kept my lips glued shut.

Half an hour later, we sat in the car, gazing at an expanse of concrete. A car park.

"Are you sure this is the right address?" Conner ran his hands along the steering wheel, up and down, up and down.

"I'm afraid so." Disappointment weighed on Mum, rounding her shoulders. Even her hair seemed to slump.

As a realtor, I could guess what had happened. The tiny, older cottages had become a money pit, or been condemned, or had been otherwise deemed less useful than premium parking space.

I pinched the key on my necklace. A key to nothing.

"Let's go back, then," I said.

Conner rolled down his window. "Or you could stretch your legs. Go for a short walk."

I didn't want to, but one look at Iris's drawn expression had me agreeing to the idea. "Sure. We can still see the water. What river is that, Mum?" I hadn't decided to call her Mum. It slipped out, but it felt right.

Iris blinked watery eyes at me. "It's a tributary of the Stour. Do you remember it?"

"I remember ducks."

Conner waited in the car, his idea, as Iris and I picked our slow way to the water with me hovering at her side, waiting to catch her if she fell.

Three feet or so back from the stones lining the waterway, we stopped.

Cool river-breeze kissed my cheeks even as it sent tendrils of my wayward hair in motion. "It's nice here."

The water amplified voices and traffic noise. Not like the bayous back home, where wildlife ruled and it got so quiet you could hear the splash of a turtle.

Iris pointed. "The cottage was over there. Remember?"

"I was only four." My tone sounded off, and I injected warmth into it. "Mostly I remember cheese sandwiches. And strips of toast dipped in soft-boiled eggs."

"You did love your toast soldiers. The egg, not so much."

"I liked the yellow fine."

We both laughed at that.

The crutches wobbled. There wasn't a bench in sight.

I held her elbow. "Shall we go back?"

"I suppose. I'm sorry the cottage isn't here anymore."

"Not your fault. Must make way for progress." I hated the flippant way the statement had come out, but it couldn't be reeled back in. And it was true, wasn't it? The past was gone.

---

To make up for my casual remark and the general grumpiness I felt was oozing out of my pores, I did my best to engage Iris on the way back, leaving Conner to concentrate on the road.

About halfway back to Parks Manor, Conner interrupted Iris's and my conversation about a deer we'd spotted on the side of the road.

"Sandy, do you have your seatbelt on?"

"What? Why?"

"The car isn't handling right."

We topped a hill, and the car picked up speed. Iris cast a worried glance at me.

In a classic over-acting job, I scrunched my nose. "Probably a minor thing. The car's been checked recently."

More car trouble wasn't likely, unless bad guys were after you.

"Conner's a great driver," I said, over the rushing sound filling my ears. "But safety first. Are you buckled, Iris?"

Conner clipped out, "The brakes aren't responding as they should. I'm going to stop as soon as I can."

"Conner," I whispered. "You're not wearing your safety belt."

A big green work truck traveled down a road to the right, heading for the intersection ahead, heedless of our car barreling down the hill. I jammed the metal of my seat buckle into the fastener and sat back, bracing myself. The truck pulled onto the lane in front of us. Conner swerved. I screamed.

The car rolled, and the world turned upside down.

## Chapter Twenty-Seven

*June 6, MONDAY 4:00 P.M.*

Hard surface underneath me. I lay flat on my back. Outside. The car had wrecked.

Iris! I jerked to a sitting position, and lightning bolts of pain shot from my left shoulder to my fingertips. My vision darkened. I swayed.

A gentle hand steadied me. "Hold on there, miss. You took a knock."

I blinked at a young man, a stranger. "How? What happened? How did I get here?"

Sirens bleated in the distance.

"The driver got you out, miss."

*Conner.*

"Where is he? Where's my mum?"

Panicked, I shot a glance past the man, but Iris and Conner were nowhere to be seen. The rear of the car angled out of a ditch. I couldn't see the rest. Ignoring the good Samaritan, I scrambled to my feet and lurched toward the vehicle. Conner and a third man were tugging at the passenger door.

Iris was in the car.

*Oh Lord, please help my mother. Let her be safe.*

A twist of black smoke escaped from under the crumpled front hood. My knees almost buckled, but I refused to collapse.

I screamed, "Get her out!"

Why hadn't I been warmer to her? Why had I thought there would be more time to talk with her? Time was never guaranteed.

Conner wrenched the door open and lifted Iris out. Holding her against his chest, he ran toward me, the whites of his terrified eyes gleaming in his blood-splattered face. The other man ran alongside. A rush of strangers met Conner and helped him take Iris, limp as a rag doll, a safe distance from the car.

Sirens came closer, filling my head, and then the emergency personnel vehicles were there, spilling out uniformed medics.

Cradling my left arm, I bent over and vomited onto the ground.

---

At the emergency room, I lay on a hard ER bed, Iris in the next one over, hooked up to IV fluids. A nasty forehead knot turning blue stood out in her ghostly-pale complexion. Other than that, she'd checked out fine, but she'd be staying for observation.

It could've been so much worse.

*Thank you, God, for protecting her.*

A nurse trotted over and checked Iris's vitals. My arm throbbed. Not as bad as before. It had been dislocated, an experience I didn't care to repeat.

## The Key Collector's Promise

As for Conner, he got five stitches to a gash in his eyebrow, the source of all the blood. He'd been tended to and promptly led away to fill out paperwork.

I heard Christine before I saw her, a strident voice above the ER clatter.

A moment later, there she was, stalking toward me, red-faced and breathing fire. "Why did you take her out? You claimed she was in danger, and I see you were right. Danger from you."

Couldn't argue with her there.

She hissed, "Stay away from my mum. You don't belong here."

A nurse nearby put down the chart she'd been holding and came to Iris's side, checking the drip in the IV. She glanced up at Christine. "Is there a problem here?"

"Yes." Christine glowered at me. "This woman has no right to be with my mum. She's nobody to us."

Iris gave a weak protest, a single uttering of Christine's name.

The nurse said, "Both the ladies are receiving treatment at present, and the officer will want to speak with them soon."

"I can wait somewhere else." Ignoring the weakness in my legs, and Iris's soft protests, I headed for a hard plastic chair in the far corner of the room.

Christine was right. I never should have taken my mother out.

I was sitting in the same chair, waiting for someone to tell me what to do, when Conner found me. Black sutures held the blood-crusted gash on his eyebrow closed, and a multitude of tiny cuts marred his good looks.

He picked up my hand and kissed my palm. "I swear, Sandy, the brakes were fine, and then they weren't."

I ran a finger across one of the cuts on his cheek. "It wasn't your fault."

No, it wasn't his fault. It was mine.

"I called Whit."

The stab of anxiety barely registered.

"The investigator wants to speak with us." He flicked a glance to Iris and took in Christine guarding her. "Come on."

Walking the plank couldn't have been harder. Every suspicion I'd had would come out now, as well as me keeping information about the second note to myself. Conner wouldn't want to hold my hand anymore, and Iris would be glad to have me exit her life again, and Daddy? No way could I keep all this from him. I shuddered. Whatever happened after this, he wouldn't be happy.

The constable led us to a small exam room with three chairs.

Conner gave his statement first, describing losing control of the vehicle when the brakes gave out and crashing, finishing with, "There've been a lot of strange things going on involving Sandra, but I'll leave the rest for her to tell."

And tell I did.

This time, I gave the police all the information I had: my unease with Daddy's dealings with Strickland and the rumors about the man, the original letter, finding the back door of number five Sycamore open when I knew I'd locked it.

As the story unfolded, Conner withdrew, not so much physically, although his posture became rigid and he crossed his

## The Key Collector's Promise

arms. A palpable coolness dropped over him when I admitted I'd purposely withheld the break-in note. He could've been made of stone, hard as any marble found in the graveyard.

At the end of my telling, the constable gave me a stern look. "I see. Any other incidents you've forgotten to mention, Miss Lejeune?"

I felt like a chewed-up wad of gum. I shook my head.

"What about my mother? Will she be safe?"

"An officer will be assigned as protection detail to watch over her until the investigation is complete."

An extra level of security sounded good. Why had I let emotion override good sense and taken Iris out? Christine would hate me forever. Some daughter I was.

After that, I answered a long list of questions, and had to give him Harriet's and Liam's contact information, even though it was on record from the night of the break-in at Sycamore Street. I inwardly groaned. Harriet would be upset with me as well.

The constable said, "That's all for now, but make yourself available for additional questions in future. Don't leave the area."

I gulped and nodded.

His tone wasn't as reprimanding when he said to Conner, "Same for you, Mr. Harris, if you don't mind."

"Of course." A muscle in Conner's jaw worked.

As soon as the door closed behind the constable, I said, "Conner, I'm sorry."

His brown eyes were chips of obsidian, hard and cold. I'd never seen him so angry. After a beat, he gave a stiff nod. That was all.

I'd lost him.

We hadn't yet left the hospital when news came about the car. The wreckage revealed a damaged brake line.

Sabotaged. It finally hit home. All this time I'd insisted my mother was the only one in danger, but no one would've expected her to be in my car.

Someone was trying to kill me.

My body shook uncontrollably, and my heart cried out for one person.

I wanted my father.

Daddy might demand explanations and subject me to recriminations but I knew, deep in my gut, he would never do anything to injure me. I finally had my answer.

The fear I had of him wasn't the fear the letter writer had instigated. I might have to face his anger, but whoever was plotting against me would face his wrath.

And if Daddy were involved in any way, he'd fix it.

# Chapter Twenty-Eight

*June 7, TUESDAY 10:00 A.M.*

A spatula-wielding Conner attacked the pancakes he was cooking for my breakfast. Other than informing me of the extra security Daddy had hired to supplement the officers patrolling the neighborhood, Conner had barely spoken to me since we'd gotten home from the hospital the day before.

Not that I could blame him.

I sat at the kitchen table, groggy from a lack of sleep and sore from our misadventure. Fatigue hadn't overridden fear until around seven, long after sunrise, and I hadn't slept long, waking with my heart pounding.

A full palette of purple and blue bruises, plus red marks, colored Conner's face.

He growled, "You should've told me about the second note. How am I supposed to keep you safe?"

I wanted to say I didn't need him to keep me safe, but truth was, I did.

"I'm sorry," I said for the thousandth time. Oscar had been lying on my right foot and pushed closer.

"Why didn't you? Tell me, I mean? I think I've earned your trust."

I almost said sorry again but swallowed it back. During the long night, I'd asked myself the same questions. If I'd ever truly suspected Conner, those suspicions had been put to rest shortly after he'd arrived. What was wrong with me? Had it really taken him saving my mother?

"I trust you."

"Right." He flipped an undercooked pancake, and it landed half-in half-out of the skillet. "Any other secrets you're keeping?"

Only my previous suspicions about Daddy. I wasn't dragging Conner into that.

Conner had already heard me tell the police about the private eye, but I offered up a crumb. "I'm not a hundred percent sure Harlow Brushy isn't connected to Strickland somehow."

This earned me one of his signature grunts. "Next time you get an anonymous threatening letter, maybe call the police instead of playing detective."

"I was worried Daddy would get in trouble." I ran my finger around the rim of my cup.

"Why don't you have a griddle, anyway?"

It looked like I wasn't the only one who didn't want to wade into those particular waters.

As he puttered about the kitchen, Conner lost a fraction of his stiffness. Every so often, he grumbled under his breath. I caught, "people who act like they know everything" and "nothing more troublesome than a Louisiana woman." I should've taken offense, but couldn't figure out if I should be insulted that he ignored my English heritage, disparaged my

## The Key Collector's Promise

Louisiana roots, had cast personal aspersions on me as troublesome, or at the general insult to my gender. Plus, he was cooking for me, a task I'd be hard put to achieve with my shoulder bruised and my arm in a sling. It seemed wiser to let his grumpiness pass.

He clonked a plate down in front of me and went back to the stove. The pancakes were burnt on the outside and raw in the middle, but I ate them anyway, the whole time craving Mrs. Ferryman's Italian coffee and famous scones. Surreptitiously, I broke off a bit of pancake and offered it to the dog under the table. He sniffed it and whined.

Conner ate standing at the counter, peering out of the window rather than joining me. At first, I thought he was simply avoiding me, but his rigid back and wide-planted feet signaled alertness.

The hairs on the back of my neck prickled. "Is someone out there?"

He turned around. "Just the security guard."

With all the watchful eyes and all of my concerns out in the open now, I should be more secure. Why did I feel the exact opposite?

I carried my plate to the sink and placed it under the tap. As awkward as it was with one arm in a sling, I picked up a sponge and dabbed at the sticky plate rather than ask Conner for help, considering his current mood.

"Let me." A scowling Conner took the sponge.

I didn't argue, just went upstairs to my bedroom. The old Bible sat on the windowsill, reminding me of Harriet, another person I'd have to confess to.

I carried the Bible to the bed. When we'd been in the accident, a prayer calling for help had come naturally, an odd thing for me. I frowned. Why had I been able to pray without hesitation? I stroked the battered cover of the Bible. Maybe because I'd been reading scripture?

Or maybe because I'd never been in a situation so fraught with danger, prayer had been instinctive. After all, I wasn't a heathen. I'd had some religious training and even walked the aisle at VBS. Been baptized. Had a certificate and everything, but more than any of that, my ten-year-old self had truly believed. I'd never really lost my belief in Jesus. I'd simply grown up. When I was a child, I'd prayed for my mother to come get me, for mean girls to leave me alone, and for Daddy to be happy. I thought I trusted God, but did I really? And if I did trust God, wouldn't I trust He heard my prayers? Just because I didn't get a yes didn't mean He didn't hear.

A frayed blue ribbon marked a spot in the Bible.

*Seeing then that we have a great high priest, that is passed into the heavens, Jesus the Son of God, let us hold fast our profession. For we have not an high priest which cannot be touched with the feeling of our infirmities; but was in all points tempted like as we are, yet without sin. Let us therefore come boldly unto the throne of grace, that we may obtain mercy, and find grace to help in time of need. Hebrews 4: 14-16 KJV*

I didn't understand all the verses, but I knew Jesus had suffered. He understood. Because of Jesus, I could pray. Tears pricked my eyes.

I lifted my good wrist, brushing my wet cheeks.

Approach the throne of grace boldly.

With a bold assurance that He understood and heard, not cocky and demanding, but with an unafraid and trusting confidence.

## The Key Collector's Promise

The puzzle pieces clicked into place. I didn't need a formula, or to check off boxes before I could come to God with my troubles. All I needed was to trust. He would hear me.

I bowed my head, not beaten down, but in reverence.

*Oh Lord,*

*I've made a mess trying to fix things on my own. Please help.*

---

Later that afternoon, the walls of the small house crowded me. At the same time, the wide-open view of a robin's-egg blue sky spotted with white, fluffy clouds taunted. Trapped inside and antsy, I neatened the bedclothes despite my bum arm, folded and refolded my laundry, and then wandered downstairs to see what else I could do.

Conner found me trying to sweep one-handed. "Give me that." Limping, he made a pass over the floor, leaving more trash behind than I had. He rolled a shoulder and stretched his neck while trying to hide a grimace.

When he caught me watching, he shot daggers. It didn't scare me. Sore myself, I eased the dustpan onto the floor, and he swept the pile of debris into it.

What a pair we were.

The floor didn't look any better, but I didn't care.

For something to say, I blurted, "Do you want something to eat?"

Surprise arched his eyebrows. "Are you hungry already?"

I shook my head.

Why hadn't I gotten a TV for this house? I sighed. Some music videos would lighten the mood.

Organizing the sparse contents of the kitchen cabinets took about twenty minutes, max.

I'd removed two of the couch cushions when Conner said, "Come on. We're going for a walk."

"But …"

"We won't go far. We'll take Oscar."

I opened my mouth to protest.

He added, "And one of the security guys."

Ever since we'd talked to the police, he'd avoided looking me straight on, but he did now. The emotion in those dark brown eyes remained unreadable to me. Not anger, at least. Haggard lines bracketed his mouth, a full, pouty-lipped mouth I had the urge to kiss until he forgot how I had hurt him. The thought shocked me. Conner was easy on the eyes, but we'd barely kissed before he'd lost interest.

"Well. What about it?" He crossed his arms. "If you keep roaming this tiny box, I'll lose my mind."

Irritation. That's what he felt for me.

"Why did you come over here to find me?" The question popped out before I thought better of it.

In two steps, he invaded my space, not threatening, but dangerous for sure. This man could do serious damage to a girl's pride, and her heart. Electricity sparked between us, setting my nerve endings alight. "Sandra, for such a smart woman, you sure can be a little slow."

Then he kissed me. And heaven help me, I kissed him back.

When we came up for air, I said, "You didn't answer my question."

"Question?" He brushed my hair behind my ear, not focusing on my words, his fingers gently tugging at my earlobe.

The small touch sent a ripple of pleasure along my spine, or maybe my reaction came from the hungry look he gave me.

What was the question? I tore my gaze away from his face.

"Why did you come?"

"Because I can't do without you, Sandra. Don't you know that?"

"Well, you did all right without me back in Louisiana."

He stepped back, all expression leaving his face. "I deserved that."

"What happened with us?"

"It sounds stupid. I wanted to have something to offer you in my own right, not have you think I was after you because you were the boss's daughter." He gave a heavy sigh. "And then we were rivals. I thought I had to earn your respect."

"I respect you." Even as I said it, I recalled the competition between us, the not-so-friendly gloating when I one-upped him. I amended, "Maybe I was too much into winning."

Or too worried about making Daddy proud. Wasn't a need to earn Daddy's approval the exact thing that bothered me most about Conner?

"But I respect you, Conner. You've been here for me. You saved my mother. Stood by me. You're exactly the kind of man I want."

"Really?" He slid his hands down my arms and back up again.

"But I am who I am. I'm competitive. Some would say aggressive. I like winning. I can't change. I won't."

The corner of his mouth lifted. "Wouldn't have it any other way."

Then that mouth came down hard on mine, and all thoughts of who was winning scattered like dandelion fluff in a gale.

## Chapter Twenty-Nine

*June 7, WEDNESDAY Afternoon*

The kiss didn't fix everything. Maybe it didn't fix anything, but we had started towards understanding each other better.

As we picked our way across the back garden and headed toward the beach with the security guy following us, Conner told me about his family and about growing up in South Louisiana. I reciprocated, talking about growing up as an only child and confessing my secret, teenage desire to be a rock star, never mind I couldn't carry a tune in a bucket and had failed at piano lessons twice.

The curtains in number four twitched, and Amy's face appeared, her expression unreadable.

I nudged Conner. "We're onstage, front and center." My chuckle held no humor.

"At least we know people are keeping an eye out."

I supposed it was good so many took the danger seriously and were watching. In judgment or sympathy, I didn't know, and was surprised to find I cared a great deal about what the honest village neighbors thought.

Oscar ran ahead, barking at the birds, sticking his nose in the water before jumping back, and generally enjoying himself. I should've taken him to run the beach outside my backdoor before.

A scrubby tree clung to a grassy hillock, and at its base, I stumbled.

"Watch it." Conner took my hand and helped me over.

His grip loosened when the earth gave way to beach, but I didn't let go. We walked, grit, pebbles and sand under our shoes, not talking. Waves hushed the household noises from my neighbors. I stopped and looked at the sea, the first time I'd done so since arriving in Suffolk. The water stretched out, unforgiving and vast, a terrible, mysterious beauty. It would be foolish for a novice sailor to venture far.

Giving my hand a final squeeze, Conner let go. When I reached to reclaim the warmth of his palm on mine, he pointed his chin down the beach.

"Your friend."

Heading toward us, Harriet stepped over a piece of flotsam on the sand. A sea breeze tossed her pale hair into a fuzzy halo. She stopped and waved a short acknowledgement, uncharacteristically abrupt.

Conner tapped me on the back. "Go talk to her."

He motioned to the security guard, met and said something to him, then jogged after the dog.

I knew the police had informed Harriet and Liam, the Ferrymans, and my other close neighbors of the situation, and it was impossible not to notice the two police vehicles stationed on the street for security.

## The Key Collector's Promise

Sand flew from Harriet's every footstep, and as she grew closer, I made out her frown. If she'd been on solid pavement, I suspect she would've been stomping.

Instead of calling out, she kept her mouth shut, her lips a tight line. Three feet away from me she came to an abrupt halt and crossed her arms, a gesture I'd seen her use on little brother Kenny. I felt five years old, cowed by the full force of her disapproval.

"The police have been questioning us. Mum's a wreck and so is Kenny. I'm trusting that you had reason not to tell me everything."

"I do. Did."

Harriet led the way to a big rock and sat, as regal as any queen in her castle and gestured for me to do likewise catty-corner to her. I sat, facing her at an angle.

Soft, gentle Harriet had transformed into a dignified force.

I met her gaze straight on, praying I could salvage our friendship. "I made a mistake."

Harriet snorted, yet somehow remained regal.

"I never would've put Kenny in danger, or Jen, or any of you. Not intentionally."

"You think that's why I'm chasing you down the beach? I knew that. Liam made it clear. What were your words? Oh, yes. 'This house is off limits'." She threw her hands in the air. "You should've told me about the note from the break-in."

"I didn't think whoever wrote it would harm Kenny or you."

Harriet pressed her fingers to her temples. "You aren't listening. What about you? Or your mother? Clearly, you took all of this seriously, or you wouldn't have come to England."

165

"I was afraid it would go badly for my father if I said anything. I thought I could handle it on my own."

"Do you see what handling it on your own resulted in?"

"I do."

Harriet softened. "Well. Just so you know, you have friends here." She shook her finger at me. "And don't you forget it."

When Conner and I made our way back to the house, the neighborhood black cat waited on the back patio stones, swishing his tail and watching me with his knowing eyes.

I put one foot on the stones. The cat hissed and let out a low growl.

Conner shooed him away. "Go on, cat."

With another swish of his tail, the cat darted away, past Oscar, who paid him no mind. Apparently, the two had made peace. Maybe reconciliation was in the air.

If only it would stay and help me deal with Daddy. I shivered, certain no cure for my fractured relationship with my father wafted on a sea breeze.

The travel time from Louisiana to the UK—not to mention the police back home in the States wanting to talk with him—left time for me to fret about Daddy's arrival, and anxiety overshadowed my initial relief at his coming.

I had a lot of explaining to do.

## Chapter Thirty

*June 8, WEDNESDAY Afternoon*

I popped another antacid, wondering how long it took to develop a full-blown ulcer, and strode to the front window. With my good arm, I twitched the semi-sheer curtains Conner had hung, debating on whether to open them to let more light in, or leave them drawn, hoping to conceal the frayed condition of the not-yet-replaced carpet.

Like a worried old man, Conner furrowed his brow and assessed me with a fretful look. "Are you sure you don't want to come with me to the airport?"

I crunched down on the chalky tablet. "It might be best if I waited here."

Daddy wouldn't blow up in public, but he had a talent for cooling a room ten degrees without a word. I shivered. Being trapped in a car with him on the trip from Heathrow? No thanks.

I said, "Maybe you could talk him down on the way here." Instead of the light hearted nonchalance I meant to project, my words had the stink of desperation.

Conner's shoulders rose and fell. He studied the carpet. "I'll try."

He took one of the security guys with him, but the other remained on duty and circled the house, the picture of alertness, easy to peg as an off-duty officer. His casual blue jeans and polo were a poor disguise and wouldn't fool anyone.

While I waited on Conner and Daddy to arrive, I wiped out the already sparkling bathroom sink, then, as best I could with one hand, began spritzing all the mirrors with glass cleaner and eradicating streaks with a crumpled newspaper.

Oscar tore to the door, barking his head off about the same time someone knocked, and I fumbled with the bottle of cleaner.

Daddy and Conner couldn't be here already.

Frowning, I stowed the bottle and newspaper in a nearby cupboard and hurried to the window. I peeked out. The security guy stood there and beside him was…Addie? Gratefulness rushed over me, turning my legs to noodles. Addie was here. She'd come with Daddy. I strained to catch sight of him, but didn't see him anywhere. The yapping dog ran in circles around me, almost tripping me as I opened the door.

He darted out and Addie shrank from him. Her palms went to her cheeks and she stepped back. Bad enough she'd been greeted by security. Now a ball of fur bowled her over.

"Oscar!" I stamped my foot. "Stop it!"

He sat and yipped at Addie, making her jump.

I turned to the security guy. "This is Addie, a family friend. The dog seems to be too rambunctious just now. Would you mind putting him in the back garden?"

He pressed his lips into a thin line. Dog duty was beneath him, but it wasn't like I could catch Oscar one-handed. He grabbed the dog by the collar, coaxing him along. I yelled a thank you.

"Goodness." Addie patted her chest.

"I'm sorry. He just gets excited."

He didn't usually. Only when chasing the cat. Maybe the dog had smelled Addie's cat on her clothes.

"How are you here? You didn't need to come."

"When I heard about the crash, nothing could keep me away."

I gave her a hug. "Addie, I'm so glad to see you. Where's Daddy?"

"They're getting the luggage. There was some delay or other. I came ahead to warn you. Your father is fit to be tied. Oh, Sandra. What sort of trouble have you got yourself into?"

And there I was, ten years old again and caught out, Addie running interference with Daddy. Heat flooded my cheeks.

Addie smoothed her hair. Her coif wasn't as neat as usual. Understandable, after a long flight from Louisiana to London.

She said, "Your father is furious. What's going on? Tell me all and I'll try to smooth the way before he skins you alive."

"What did Daddy say?"

"Not much. You'll have to fill me in." Her mouth puckered in sympathy as she took in my sling. "Does it hurt?"

"Not much."

"You poor thing. And look at your face!"

I touched my cheek. I'd almost forgotten the few bruises I'd sustained. They were nothing compared to Conner's.

"I'm fine, Addie." I bit my bottom lip.

Addie clucked her tongue. "You most certainly are not. I'm making you a cup of tea. Isn't that what we do here? When in Rome? Or England, as it were."

She tittered at her own joke, and I joined in with a weak chuckle.

In typical Addie fashion, she steered me to the table, commanding me to sit, while she bustled around the kitchen, turning on the kettle and collecting mugs. "So what's all this about a note?"

I started at the beginning, giving her the short version, leaving out my suspicions against Conner, and Daddy.

"Go ahead and let it all out while I tend to the tea. I'm listening."

I knew she was. The cozy kitchen, with Addie brewing tea, gathering my two pretty cups and saucers, and setting out scones on paper towels, reminded me of past days when I'd spill my deepest concerns to her, only the snacks were different then, milk and donuts.

Addie set a saucer and a full cup before me and took a seat opposite.

I took a swallow of the tea. It was oversweet, and I nestled the cup back into its saucer. "I never wanted Daddy to partner with Mr. Strickland."

"I suppose that is where the trouble started." She took a sip of her tea and pointedly glanced at my cup.

Obediently, I reclaimed the cup and drank a little more, earning a pleased smile from Addie.

She said, "Do you have the letter here?"

"The police have it."

Oscar whined outside the back door and scratched to be let in.

I said, "I'd better see what's wrong with the dog. He doesn't usually cry like that."

For a second, I could've sworn Addie's features contorted in a flash of anger, but it was gone in a second, if it had even been there at all.

Did Addie dislike dogs? I'd never seen her around any pet other than her cat.

Oscar let out a cry. "He might've got into thorns or something."

I didn't wait for her permission to tend my dog. If she didn't like him being around she'd have to get over it. As soon as I let him in, he pressed against my leg and growled at Addie.

I snapped my fingers at him. "Stop that!"

He tucked his tail and gave me sad eyes but didn't slink off at my scolding. Maybe he was sick. I crouched to examine him and almost lost my balance until I grabbed hold of a chair leg for stability.

"You all right, hon?" Instead of assisting me, Addie warily eyed the situation from her seat and nibbled at her scone. She wasn't going near the dog.

"Fine. Tired, I guess." As soon as I said it, fatigue weighed on me, making my limbs awkward and heavy. "Not quite myself yet."

"I imagine so."

I smoothed the dog's fur, finding no sign of an injury, and he didn't whimper. "What's wrong, pup?"

He squirmed and put a paw on my thigh.

From my lowered position, I peered up at Addie. "I don't know what's got into him."

"No matter. Let's finish our tea."

"Not sure tea can fix today. How long before Daddy and Conner get here, do you think?" I took my seat and picked up my cup.

"With the break in, did you see anyone?"

I shook my head, and the room tipped. The cup fell from my hands. It hit the floor and shattered.

Oscar whined again.

Addie sighed. "I suppose I'll have to clean up your mess, Sandra. Isn't it what I always do? Why can't you just do what you're told?"

"Do what I'm told?" Furrowing my brow, I struggled to follow her train of thought. "What do you mean?"

"Come on." Addie hauled me up by the arm. Then she let out a yelp and released me.

I flopped back into the chair, blinking at Addie and the dog pulling her pant leg.

She hissed. "Stupid dog. I should've taken care of this mutt ages ago." She snatched a dish towel from the table, wrapped his jaws closed, and bundled him into the pantry.

"Wait a minute. You can't." My words came slow. "Don't treat my dog like that." I leaned forward but couldn't seem to get my feet under me. My muscles had turned to jelly. I frowned. Why was I so sluggish? My fuzzy brain couldn't process. Then it dawned on me.

I'd been drugged—by Addie. For what reason?

Her face a distorted mask, she loomed over me.

"Why?" I croaked out.

She snorted. "Couldn't figure it out? No surprise. You wouldn't have made it through high school without me helping you with your homework."

The jab stung. More than that, it terrified me.

This wasn't my Addie.

My heart thundered in my ears. Adrenaline pushed against whatever drug she'd dosed me with. I struggled to keep my eyes from closing. Addie dropped a coil of rope on the table. Terror clawed at my throat. I inhaled to scream, and she shoved a rag into my mouth.

"After all I've done for you and your father, do you think he'd help me out of a jam? No. Not him."

I batted at the gag with my good hand and rose from the chair.

"Oh, no you don't." As fast as any cowboy, she secured the rope around my torso, tying my arms down.

She jerked me sideways. Unbalanced, I sagged against her. My legs wouldn't work.

*Think, Sandra.*

Instead of fighting to stand, I relaxed and made myself a dead weight. Grunting and swearing, she dragged me up the stairs.

Between huffs and puffs, she said, "Then you come along and ruin my plan to feather my nest. I warned you, Sandra."

My blood ran cold. Should I make a break for it? Trussed up the way I was, I'd never get away. No. Get to the top of the stairs and then knock her down.

I let my head loll to the side. She bumped my bruised shoulder and I swallowed a groan. Three more steps.

Addie said, "It's your own fault. I never wanted this to happen. I hope you know that. If you had just left well enough alone, no one would have gotten hurt. There wouldn't have even been a car wreck. But you're so stubborn."

On the top step, I planted my feet, straightened, and shoved her with everything in me. Arms pin wheeling, she hooked one of her claws in my sling, and we both went tumbling down the staircase. Addie screamed. We hit the floor hard, me landing on top, and her scream cut off.

Fighting vertigo, I staggered to my feet and loped toward the door. The security guard rattled the knob. I'd turned the lock after Addie had come in. Even lassoed with my arms pinned, I could reach the lock, but couldn't work it. My numb hands refused to cooperate.

Trapped.

I whirled around, expecting to see Addie coming after me, but she lay unmoving where we had landed. For a second, the urge to go to her warred with my good sense.

I lurched toward the front window and ducked under the curtains, banging the glass with my forehead. The security guard saw me. His eyes widened, and he redoubled his efforts, kicking the door. Another man ran up with a crowbar.

I prayed they'd get inside before Addie came to. Bound as I was, I couldn't do much to stop her besides sit on her, which was exactly what I intended to do. The curtain clung to me and I fought it off, breaking free just as the front door splintered.

I didn't stop. I staggered to Addie and flopped onto her inert form. The minute my body made contact, I knew. The muffled cries were coming from me, not her.

Addie was gone.

# Chapter Thirty-One

*June 8, WEDNESDAY Night*

"What were you thinking?" Daddy, his white button-up wrinkled from travel and his jaw peppered with gray scruff, prowled the hospital room, raking both hands through his hair. "You scared us half to death, Sandra."

The tumble down the stairs had not only given me a new collection of bruises, it had torn ligaments in my shoulder. I'd need surgery to repair it. Pain spiked through me. No meds for me until whatever drug Addie had loaded the tea with ran through my system.

At least my sorry state kept Daddy's temper at bay, but I wished he'd stop pacing like a trapped bear. Then he did stop, turned on his heel, and stared at me. For the first time in my memory, he looked lost, and maybe even hurt. I had no defenses against it. Those piercing eyes searched me as if digging for gold nuggets of truth.

"Honestly, Sandra. Why didn't you tell me about the letter? I could've gotten to the bottom of it."

Battered and worn, I'd had enough of this game.

I sighed. "Daddy, I begged you not to go into business with Strickland. You wouldn't listen. Then the letter came and I thought it was from him. I didn't know how deep you'd gotten in. What was I supposed to do?"

A muscle in his jaw worked. "The business was failing. I needed to shore it up. For you. What kind of man leaves his child nothing?"

"Nothing? Having you safe isn't nothing, Daddy. I'm not willing to trade our safety for money."

"I'd never put you in harm's way."

"But you did."

In the terrible silence that followed, Daddy turned pale green, but he remained his stoic self, in control, as always. He said, "You're right. I made a mistake."

For years I'd waited for those words of admission. They brought no satisfaction. Small, insignificant words, not changing a thing. All they did was expose the man of clay.

We were still us. I still needed surgery. And Addie was still dead. Addie, who had stalked me and sabotaged my car.

I started to cry. "Why did Addie do it, Daddy?"

He flinched and turned his head as if I'd slapped him. I knew there was more to the story of Addie and my father. To the tips of my aching toes, I regretted hurting Addie. I loved her. And I hated her. Had anything about our relationship been real? A slideshow of memories played through my mind. Addie helping me pick out my first bra, Addie sharing her lunches with me, and later, Addie advising on how to deal with troublesome clients. Now every memory was corrupted with the knowledge that she'd had an ulterior motive.

Had my perception been off the whole time?

# The Key Collector's Promise

I couldn't do without my Addie, my rock. But it had all been an illusion. My throat burned and my heart hurt worse than any torn up shoulder or bruised hip could.

Daddy remained as silent and unmoving as a slab of concrete. His Adam's apple bobbed a few times before he finally said, "That's a conversation we can have when you're healed."

Not exactly an answer, but more than an outright refusal.

A nurse came in. "There's another visitor, but the doctor said only one at a time. A young man named Conner. Shall I send him in or ask him to wait?"

We answered at the same time.

I said, "Send him in."

Daddy said, "Tell him to wait."

Daddy hung his head, "She wants to see him. I'll go." He bent and kissed my cheek. Stroking my hair, he said, "I'll cancel the Strickland deal, but you have to do something for me."

Always with strings.

"What is it?"

His mouth worked, and he gripped my chin, forcing me to look at him. "Don't go throwing yourself into danger again. Ever." He stared at me, those glinting blue eyes boring into mine.

I swallowed hard. "I won't."

With a nod, he gave my chin a gentle pinch, let go, and stood. "You're a tough little fighter, and I couldn't be prouder of you. I'll be right outside."

I wanted to hold on to the praise, to cherish it. I'd craved it for so long, but his words slid right off the armor he'd instilled. I loved him. Admired him. But it would take more than crumbs of affirmation to win back my trust.

He crossed the room, paused at the door to arrange his clothing and straighten his posture, shoulders back, jaw rigid. I'd often done the same thing, putting on a façade before facing the world. I didn't remember Daddy doing it before, but of course he must've. No one could be as firm and confident as Daddy appeared all the time. Maybe he had always done it, and I simply hadn't paid attention.

Conner came in and held my hand while I cried. Iris was safe, but I'd lost Addie.

I didn't know what to do with that.

The damage to my shoulder and subsequent surgery required a stay in the hospital. After a week, I convinced Daddy to go home to manage things, or maybe Conner did, because he stayed, haunting the halls of the hospital and refusing to leave. Conner and Daddy were still in cahoots, but this time I didn't mind. I'd rather Conner report to Daddy than face my father's sad, confused face. Daddy had no answers for me, at least nothing he was ready to share.

At first, I leaned on Conner, but soon the attention began smothering me. When I gave him a to-do list to ready the house at number five for marketing to vacation renters, he finally left me in peace, but not before tossing me a sideways grin and peppering my cheeks with kisses.

I was healing from the surgery. The emotional wounds would take longer.

# Chapter Thirty-Two

*June 22, Two Weeks Later*

Christine had brought Iris to number five for a lunchtime visit, the three of us leaving Conner in the house as he worked on the final touches to the renovations.

Under the giant sycamore, Harriet had set out lawn chairs, and directed Iris and me to sit. She readjusted Jennifer's shirt, settling her on a red-checkered cloth. Christine squatted next to the toddler, playing peek-a-boo with her while Harriet came over to sit with me and Mum.

My cousin, or sister, or whoever she was, protected Iris with ferocity and refused to let Iris visit me without her. I could deal with that, and any of Christine's sour moods, in trade for the assurance my mother had a dependable person. I counted my blessings.

Harriet said, "Can't you stay in Eden Cove a bit longer? The house should keep you busy."

I shook my head. "I've got to get back."

"It's a lovely place to live, I promise." Harriet chewed her bottom lip.

Ducks swam in formation at the pond, and a sea breeze rustled the leaves of the sycamore tree. An idyllic scene, but I couldn't ignore facts. Many of the neighbors avoided me. Besides Jennifer, no children played outside in the grassy area, or anywhere within sight. They'd all vanished as soon as I appeared. Still, it *was* a lovely place, and they'd soon soften, once the gossip died down.

I said, "I know it is."

Harriet said, "Even if he wasn't an active participant, it was Kenny's old friends who scared you so. We all feel terrible about it."

I patted her arm. "Don't be silly. He didn't have reason to connect the break-in to his old gang."

The break-in and the mysterious note had turned out to be directed at Kenny. The trouble between Kenny and his parents had to do with Kenny's previous friends, the gang of prank-pulling boys he'd broken away from. They had seen him coming and going at number five and had planned to stir up trouble for him. When Kenny had found out about the note, he'd come forward right away about recent encounters with the other boys.

I felt the need to stick up for him. "He told us as soon as he realized it was the gang."

Iris piped up. "Well. What's done is done. Those boys won't bother you anymore. And it seems you have good neighbors here to keep a sharp lookout."

As if to prove the point, Amy, with her ever-present walking stick—one I was sure meant for defense more than anything else—emerged from number four and set off on one of her walks. She half turned and waved at us. I returned the gesture.

## The Key Collector's Promise

I said, "I have to go back. Clients."

No doubt my clients could find another realtor. It was tempting to stay tucked away in Eden Cove and not deal with Daddy, or the fallout from Addie's mess, but he'd asked me to come home and help him salvage Lejeune Reality. I'd prayed long and hard over it. Daddy was stubborn and difficult, a deeply flawed man, but he was my father. I loved him.

I couldn't walk away from him.

A gust of wind stirred the tree's leaves. Harriet tucked her hair behind her ear. "I hope you'll come back."

Iris's face puckered up and she bent her head down, adjusting a button on her cardigan that didn't need adjusting at all. She murmured, "I hope so, too." She brought her gaze up.

Looking her dead on, I took her hands in mine and gave them a gentle squeeze. "I have to go home, but I'll come back. I promise. And you promise to write me."

She gave me a watery smile, and I released her.

My fingers went to the key I still wore on its chain. Impulsively, I took it off and fastened it around her neck. "So you won't forget."

With a quick inhalation of breath, she placed a hand flat on her chest, the key underneath her palm. "Never. I'll never forget. I promise."

I breathed in the salty air, ate my sandwich, and enjoyed the day with my company. Conner joined us. All too soon, it was time for Iris to go. To my surprise, Christine gave me a stiff side hug.

She said, "Ring me when you get back to Eden Cove and I'll bring Mum round."

Christine pinned me with a look. We both knew Iris's health held no guarantees. Christine was setting aside any misgivings she had about me and asking me to return soon.

I nodded. "I will."

As they motored away, Conner put his arm around me. I kept a smile on my face and waved until their car got to the end of Sycamore Street.

Conner rubbed my back. "We better take Oscar over to Harriet's."

"Could you?" I couldn't handle another goodbye. "I'm beat."

"Sure." He kissed me on the forehead.

He called the dog and I went upstairs to my bedroom, the last room we'd painted. The secondhand dresser, a new mattress with its mint green bedding, and contemporary wall art finished out the room, ready for the vacation renters I hoped to sign on.

Conner and I would be bound for Louisiana in a few hours. I'd packed almost everything ahead of time. It wasn't much, but more than I came with. During my hospital stay, Iris had gifted me with three suitable nightgowns, a robe, and fuzzy slippers. Kenny had made me a wooden picture frame and Harriet had painted it with tiny flowers and hearts. Inside was a picture of me with Harriet and Jennifer in front of her house. I wrapped it in a T-shirt and tucked it securely amongst the packed clothing.

Several packets of photos from the one-hour developer sat on the dresser. During my convalescence at number five, Conner and I had taken tons of pictures of the local scenery with a cheap 110 camera he'd bought, his attempt to distract me from my grief. I'd feigned interest in the castle ruins and other sights, but my heart hadn't been in it.

## The Key Collector's Promise

A small stack of books Conner had bought while I was in the hospital sat atop the dresser as well, along with the found copy of *The Last of the Mohicans*, the only book I'd take with me. The rest were too heavy to pack. I'd leave them on the downstairs bookshelves he and Liam had crafted. For now, number five would be a cozy spot for a lucky, short-term renter.

I already missed the place.

The half-open window let in a warm breeze and I crossed the room, intending to open it all the way. The strains of a guitar playing drifted through and I stilled. A crooning male voice began. Kenny singing *Make My Life a Prayer*.

I'm not sure how long I stood there, listening to Kenny sing about God's patience and of His comfort.

How did a person make their life a prayer? According to the song, trust and believe. Sounded simple, but trusting and believing wasn't always easy.

I still stumbled through prayers, didn't know the right words to use, and forgot to pray sometimes, but I no longer felt lost, or like I needed to run through obstacles to find God. I only needed to run to Him.

He understood.

How it all worked was a mystery, but I knew part of the work was believing God heard my prayers, and believing He loved me.

Trust and believe.

## Chapter Thirty-Three

*July*

Back home, I clung to what I knew was true. The more I prayed, the more snippets of my past faith returned, helping me find my footing on hazardous terrain.

Addie had no family. I'd known that, but not even a distant relative came forward to claim her. And then we found out she'd left everything to me, all thirty-seven dollars and fifty-six cents, and her sprawling old ancestral home, mortgaged to the hilt and then some. Addie had been playing a dangerous game, gambling with her finances and losing big.

Only after the reading of the will did Daddy let me in on just how much he depended on Addie's advice. She'd encouraged him to consider the Strickland deal, possibly arranged it. Without the deal, she'd been certain to lose the house that had been in her family for generations.

The will had been drawn up years before, when she'd been flush.

With each disclosure, my memories of her kept reforming, trying to make sense of her actions. Addie dedicated her life to

Lejeune's only to turn on us in the end. Was it only over money?

The police didn't think so.

After they questioned Daddy, he dropped a bombshell. He and Addie had dated a few times early on, but he insisted it had ended amicably, in a friendship. I should have seen it. Addie's devotion made a twisted sort of sense if she'd been carrying a torch for him or caught up in a fantasy.

Had Daddy encouraged her?

If he had, I wasn't sure I wanted to know.

# Epilogue

*Five Years Later*

Seven-year-old Jennifer ran along the beach with Chase, my three-year-old, toddling after her.

Harriet, her blonde hair a halo around her head yelled after them. "Careful, now!"

I wasn't worried. Jennifer took her child-caring duties seriously. We came at least twice a year. Jennifer and Chase got along like cousins, even though they weren't blood-related. My stay would be longer than usual this time.

I stepped over a branch in the sand and reached for Harriet, my eight-months-pregnant belly throwing my center of gravity off.

After navigating the debris, I picked up the conversation. "How's Kenny handling college?"

He'd decided to become a doctor, a heart specialist. The whole family was bursting with pride over him.

Harriet beamed. "Doing quite well. He'll be home for a visit soon."

"Think he'll be around in three or four months?"

"I know he'd love to see you. And the new baby."

I'd stay in Eden Cove until the baby could travel. Mum hadn't been doing well, but was determined to see the new little one. I hoped having visits to look forward to would help keep her strong.

Over time, I'd teased out more of her story, sparking a few memories of my own of a man I'd called Jeff. In my mind, I'd thought him a gardener, because he'd brought flowers to the cottage. I should've gotten mad when I realized that back then, my mother had taken four-year-old me with her to meet her boyfriend, but it was impossible to merge the two versions of my mother. Those past days seemed like ancient history. Still, when I looked at my own child, it was easy to imagine how Daddy must've felt when he found the cottage. He'd punched the guy, taken me, and filed for divorce. Not his best moment, he admitted, when I confronted him.

On the beach, Chase stumbled and flopped onto his knees. Jennifer helped him up and brushed sand away, but he was having none of it. Crying, he did an about face and ran toward me.

I cupped my hands around my mouth. "Look at the birds, Chase." I pointed to the gulls circling in the blue sky.

He stopped and tipped his head back. Jennifer crouched beside him and pointed.

Harriet said, "Do you think you'll ever stay in Eden Cove for good?"

I sighed. "We love it here, but Conner is doing well with business back home. Maybe if I continue acquiring rental properties here, we can base the business in the UK. Someday."

Christine, of all people, had helped me find investment properties. Now I had several, with her as manager while I was in Louisiana. We'd made a good team, only occasionally needing Conner to referee.

I smiled wryly. "Although how Daddy could do without Chase to spoil I don't know." I touched my protruding belly. "And this little one."

In his role as papaw, Daddy had lost all his sharp edges. He spoiled Chase horribly. He'd become both softer toward me and more querulous, but never had a cross word for Chase, whom he adored. I couldn't take Chase from his papaw, and papaw wasn't inclined to take to the English countryside.

Harriet pulled at the waistband of her shorts, noticeably loose. She'd lost weight since I saw her last.

A cheery whistle pierced the air.

My husband.

Chase dropped the stick he'd been poking into the sand and headed for us, or more accurately, to his daddy behind us. I couldn't help it, I turned around. Conner strolled toward us, his normal hurried pace slowed to account for Oscar. He'd become Kenny's dog, but never failed to return for belly rubs and kibble every time I visited Eden Cove.

Harriet shaded her eyes and motioned for Jennifer to hurry and join us. "Are you sure you're all right to trek to the ruins?"

I laughed and was about to tell her I was pregnant, not sick, but caught myself in time.

She hadn't said she wanted more babies, but she loved them, and there hadn't been another. Maybe I should spend more time in Eden Cove after my little one came.

I said, "It will be fine. Conner will carry me back if I show the least sign of getting tired."

Harriet grinned the grin that lit up her face. "I'm sure he will. He's a good man, your Conner."

## The Key Collector's Promise

He was. He really was.

When he caught up to us, he kissed me, and I kissed him back before gently shoving him away.

"Behave yourself, husband."

"Too late." He winked.

As he jogged off toward our son, I took Harriet's hand, and we walked toward our children. Later, after I'd been to see Mum for as long as Chase allowed, we would come back to Eden Cove for dinner at Harriet's, Bubble and Squeak, a dish of potatoes, cabbage, and other wonderful things fried up. I'd see Liam and some of the other neighbors. In the morning, we'd have scones and Italian coffee at the bakery. Then we'd go to church.

I touched my necklace, a plain cross. I'd never outgrown the habit of reaching for the key. That had been about a promise I made to my mother.

The cross reminded me about other promises. Those from God to me, and those I'd made to Him.

*Dear Reader,*

*I hope you enjoyed your time in Eden Cove reading about Sandra's story. Thank you for reading.*

*All my best,*

*Donna Jo*

Customer reviews help indie authors get noticed and allow them to continue sharing their stories. Readers can leave a review on Amazon or any of their preferred platforms.

**Scan the QR code to sign up for Donna Jo's Newsletter**

**or go to donnajostone.com**

Enjoy a sneak peek of...
# The MAESTRO'S MISSING MELODY

*Amy Walsh*

Donna Jo Stone

# Chapter One

"I have to get out *here?*" I gasped as I peered through the pouring rain to the winding drive leading uphill to St. Bartholomew's Church. Of course, in my rush to return to the taxi, I'd left my travel umbrella behind at Petal Cottage.

"Sorry, but there's no way I can get closer," the driver said. He gestured toward the street ahead. "Those cars aren't moving. People in Eden Cove park right on the drive for church gatherings—always have. Small parking lot."

I pulled the disposable poncho Gran had insisted I pack from its vinyl envelope, unfolded it, and pulled it over my head. "Nothing you can do, so no worries. Thanks for the lift." I forced a smile while swiping my card through the payment box.

Climbing out of the cab, I bent my head so the flimsy poncho hood would hang over my face as I zigzagged between cars. I certainly didn't want mascara trails running down my cheeks if I met the maestro for the first time.

By the time I reached the church, I was chuffing like the *Little Engine That Could*, even though Gramps would say the hill was a hummock compared to our Wyoming mountains. My trendy suede mules were now dark brown, and the formerly wispy flounces of my boho sundress trailed on the ground. I

## The Key Collector's Promise

stood in the foyer momentarily, breathing in through my nose and out through my mouth to slow my breathing.

As I pulled off the poncho, more water dripped to the floor. A rack of umbrellas was parked by the door—all dry. Everyone else must have gotten into St. Bartholomew's before the rain.

"Of course! No garbage can," I muttered as I looked for a place to dispose of the poncho.

The final warm-up began, my cue that the string quartet was about to start. *Oh no! Dripping wet and late! What a great first impression I'll make!*

I hurriedly squished the poncho into my purse. What had been a neat little square now looked like a mound of wet saran wrap hanging over both sides.

Inside, the pews were full. As a gentleman turned to address the audience, I wiggled around several pairs of knees to plunk myself into an empty spot in the direct center of one of the long seats.

The director introduced his small ensemble and apologized for not being Miss Beatrice. There was a twitter of giggles and chuckles when he said, "Today's performance surely won't be the same without her."

I concluded that Miss Beatrice must be quite a character before closing my eyes to soak in the opening bars of "Divertimento in D Major." As always, when listening to Mozart, I marveled that a mortal could write such music—that this beauty was only a glimpse of what the music of Heaven would be.

The building was like a small cathedral, with the acoustics creating the perfect linger for each note, a haunting echo not long enough to cause discordance. At one point, my purse slid to the floor, and I opened my eyes to realize my arms hovered above my lap with my hands cupped as though my ears weren't enough to capture the sound. I peeked at the middle-aged woman to my left and then the bearded man to my right. Thank goodness! Neither seemed to have noticed my weirdness.

I soon returned to being enraptured. The violins slowed down as if musing over the wonders of nature while the cello and base supported them in a comforting undertone. I had played these same notes many times on my collection of stringed instruments, but familiarity made my heart all the fonder.

Then came those precious notes of the Andante movement. Dark honey-sweet tones of the cello took the lead just as the sun began to shine through the stained glass, sending arcs of gentle greens, blues, and pinks across the young musicians' faces. For the first time, I knew one hundred percent that I was meant to be in Eden Cove. Despite all the last-minute changes in arrangements and my many traveling blunders. Despite my disappointment in not going to the Scottish Highlands of my ancestors.

Being here was God-ordained. He had planned it before I had even germinated. Just like every other blessing and trial that had formed my character. *Thank you, Father God.*

And that is when I heard the twangy "Yippie-yi-yay" of Willie Nelson, followed by the mellow "Yippie-yi-o" of Johnny Cash. Coming from below the pew. Gramp's ringtone. Full volume.

Frantically, I lifted my purse and began fishing past the soggy poncho.

"Ghost riders in. Ghost riders in the sky," Nelson and Cash sang in unison.

## The Key Collector's Promise

Suddenly, the bearded man next to me yanked my purse right out of my hands and tossed the wet wad of poncho to the floor. As he pulled my phone out of my purse, I grabbed it from him and hit the side button to silence my grandfather's favorite tune.

My face felt one hundred ten degrees. I glanced down to see if my body was shimmering with steam. Then I turned towards the man who… had tried to help me.

The small ensemble fell silent as I stared into brown eyes made beautifully golden by the sun shining through a nearby stained-glass window. It was hard to believe I could be mesmerized by those golden-browns—mesmerized enough to forget my embarrassment. But then, I've always been an eye-girl.

Amid my ogling, it struck me that I had seen the face under that beard before.

Oh crud. I was sitting next to Huntley Milne, multi-winner of the Grand Master Fiddler Championship in Nashville—and every Scots fiddle contest he deemed worthy of his expertise. Here was the man I'd wanted to meet since Gramps took me to the Rocky Mountain Fiddle Championships when I was fourteen. The maestro I was going to apprentice under for the next few weeks.

That was, *if* he would keep me in the program after my cell phone had just sabotaged the Deben Sinfonia's "Birthday of the King Extravaganza."

The imbecility of that young woman—some people were just plain ignoramuses—I was still fuming miles away from St. Bart's. She'd ruined weeks of practice. Fourteen minutes of

Mozart would have to be cut from the recording. And this might be the final performance Aunt BeeBee could take credit for. It certainly looked that way, at least.

Even Dory and David were still focused on the raucous interruption. However, unlike me, they found it hilarious. The tweens often seemed to share one mind and one sense of humor. Maybe that was normal for twins. I'd had to redirect my glare from the young hippie girl to them when their quivering and snickers continued long after she had whispered an apology and turned her body away from me in the pew.

"Wait until we tell Mama Bee about that girl's cellphone going off in the middle of the concert!" David crowed from the back seat of my Vauxhall Astra.

From the passenger seat, Dory turned toward her brother. "That was epic! So much better than if it had been a normal ringtone." The twins gave each other a high five as though they had orchestrated the untimely phone call themselves. "Yippie-yi-o," Dory deepened her voice and added some rasp. "Yippie-yi-yay."

"Who sings that, Uncle Huntley?"

"Two American singers," I muttered. "Country Western."

As I pulled into the small lot of Balmy Bay Residences, I had flashbacks of my time in Wyoming almost a decade ago. An Old-West-themed bar in Jackson. Ailsa and I line dancing to "On the Road Again." Her head thrown back in laughter every time I made a misstep. Me purposely stepping wrong just to hear that bell-like trill above Nelson's nasal baritone.

I shook off the memories as we entered the care home where my aunt had often volunteered and was now a new resident. I still wasn't clear why she'd been admitted here rather than to a hospital. She and the presiding doctor were quite good

## The Key Collector's Promise

friends, so perhaps he let her stay where she was most comfortable out of courtesy.

I followed the twins into Aunt BeeBee's room in time to hear her surprisingly unique brand of snoring for the first time.

"Zzzzz Zzzz hmm hmm. Zzzz Zzzz hmm hmm."

Dory began the same whispery giggle she'd had during the errant cellphone call, and David didn't even try to tone down his guffaw.

"It sounds like she's snoring the introduction to Beethoven's Fifth," he snorted.

Aunt BeeBee's head shook slightly, and her left eye opened, then her right. "Who are you?"

"It's me—Huntley. With Dory and David." The twins were immediately somber. Their foreheads slid into matching pleated worry lines. This wasn't good. She should have known who we were immediately.

"Ooo, yes. I know you," my aunt said. Her eyebrows shot almost to her hairline, and her upper body bounced up and down like an excited toddler's. "Did you bring me a mincemeat pie?"

"You hate mincemeat pie, Mama Bee," Dory scolded. "Don't you remember?"

"Oh, so I do. So, I do." There was a long pause. "Did you find the Milne stave book?"

"Not yet, I'm sorry," I said "I've been a bit busy."

Her forehead wrinkled with confusion. "Busy doing what?"

I couldn't hold back a sigh. My larger-than-life, metaphorically anvil-juggling aunt probably wouldn't have felt overwhelmed with all I'd had to accomplish in the past few days, but I certainly was. "It's the life of a musician. You should know we are very busy people, Aunt BeeBee."

"You have to look everywhere until you find it, Huntley."

Our visit was short. I brought the twins because they'd been asking to see her all week, but she barely interacted with them. All Aunt BeeBee could talk about was the volume of Milne scores, which she wanted me to bring to Balmy Bay the next time I visited. I hadn't even begun to look for it. I'd been busy rescheduling summer performances and rerouting the handful of interns I had agreed to teach over the summer as part of my fellowship with the Royal Conservatoire of Scotland.

Our goodbyes were painfully disjointed. My aunt said odd things, and Dory and David acted timid and awkward, even though they'd been with my aunt for a few years. In their defense, she didn't seem like the same person she was when she'd first adopted them—or even who she was when I last visited Eden Cove.

Dory sniffled all the way to the car, and thankfully, David squeezed his lanky body into the diminutive backseat to comfort her. I was glad he was such a good brother because I had no words.

"What if Mama Bee never gets better?" Dory eventually asked. "Do you think Aunt Rachelle will move back into the Monstrosity? To take care of us?"

I shrugged and mumbled, "Maybe." It was highly unlikely. BeeBee's best friend, Rachelle, had initially agreed to help her raise the twins. But then, at age seventy, she had fallen in love and moved in with her new husband.

Hadn't Aunt BeeBee told Dory and David that I had agreed to take guardianship of them should something happen to her?

## The Key Collector's Promise

When my aunt approached Aisla and me before the adoption, it had been my sweet wife who'd exuberantly promised, "Of course, we'd take them in!" before I had time to ponder.

If things had gone differently, we would have had a four-year-old squeezed in the backseat between the twins. And I would have been much more up to the task of minding children with Ailsa by my side.

Donna Jo Stone

# OUR HOUSE on Sycamore Street

Discover a tale of romance, intrigue, humour or heart behind every door.
All you have to do is knock!

OUR HOUSE on Sycamore Street

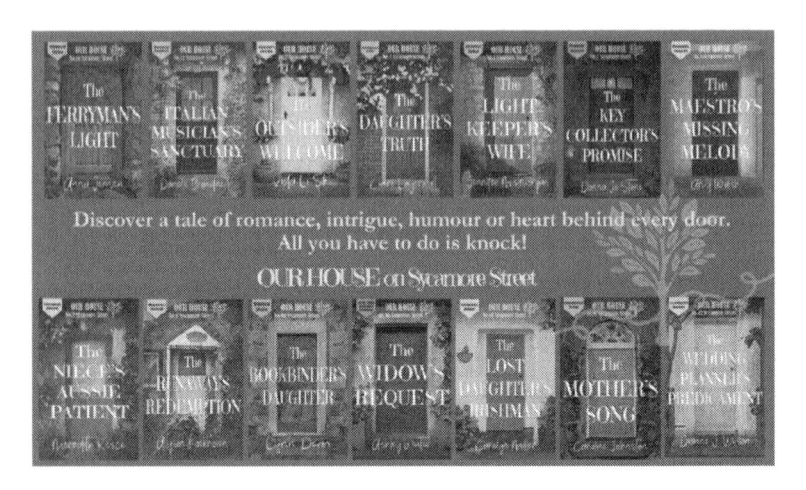

### BOOK 1: THE FERRYMAN'S LIGHT  *by Anna Jensen*
He has plans for the future. What happens when circumstances dictate those plans must change?

### BOOK 2: THE ITALIAN MUSICIAN'S SANCTUARY
*by Danielle Grandinetti*
Hunted by one man, can she open her heart to another?

### BOOK 3: THE OUTSIDER'S WELCOME
*by Vida Li Sik*
If you love women's fiction, you will enjoy The Outsider's Welcome, a tale of resilience, community, and a search for belonging.

### BOOK 4: THE DAUGHTER'S TRUTH  *by Claire Lagerwall*
Emmy Whitehouse is about to discover that everything she knows is not at all what she thinks.

## BOOK 5: THE LIGHT KEEPER'S WIFE
*by Jennifer Mistmorgan*

They've come to escape their wartime secrets. But are some shadows too dark to shake off?

## BOOK 6: THE KEY COLLECTOR'S PROMISE
*by Donna Jo Stone*

She came to warn her estranged mother of danger. But will the cost of unraveling family secrets be too much to bear?

## BOOK 7: THE MAESTRO'S MISSING MELODY
*by Amy Walsh*

She is thrilled to apprentice with her fiddler hero—until his grumpiness knocks him off his pedestal.

## BOOK 8: THE NIECE'S AUSSIE PATIENT
*by Meredith Resce*

Newly graduated in hospitality management, Stephanie Delafonte is looking forward to managing her aunt's guest house for three weeks while Lina takes a well-earned break.

## BOOK 9: THE RUNAWAY'S REDEMPTION
*by Allyson Koekhoven*

A tragic event at work leaves South African paramedic Johlene Anderson reeling.

## BOOK 10: THE BOOKBINDER'S DAUGHTER
*by Lynn Dean*

A war refugee is invited to live with an aging recluse but learns too late she's being used.

## BOOK 11: THE WIDOW'S REQUEST *by Ashley Winter*

Join Fiona as she unravels old family secrets, faces danger head on and uncovers the truth about her parents' deception...

## BOOK 12: THE LOST DAUGHTER'S IRISHMAN
*by Carolyn Miller*

She wants to find a way to live again; he wants to close a deal and move on. Until sparks fly and these opposites attract in this contemporary romance filled with heart and humour.

## BOOK 13: THE MOTHER'S SONG *by Caroline Johnston*

Miranda McVitty, wife, mother and campsite owner. Miranda loves to sing as she goes about her work and this summer she's learning to sing her prayers as well as her to do list.

## BOOK 14: THE WEDDING PLANNER'S PREDICAMENT
*by Dianne J. Wilson*

Cleo is done organizing weddings. James has a wedding to plan, and Cleo is his only hope.

# About the author

Donna Jo Stone writes southern-flavored novels for the inspirational and general market. Her stories are often about people facing tough times. Not all of her books have romance but when they do, the romances are sweet. No graphic language, sex, or violence, just plenty of heart-tugging emotion with endings that leave readers with a sense of hope.

When she's not writing or reading, she spends her time hanging out with family and friends, and occasionally visits bookshops and fabric sales.


You can learn more about Donna Jo by visiting her at https://donnajostone.com.

## More from Donna Jo Stone

Joann Apron Strings Book Five

(1960s Sweet Romance)

A Wedding to Remember

(A Bed & Breakfast Novelette)

***Coming 2024***

When the Wildflowers Bloom Again

(Historical Southern Fiction)

***Coming 2025***

Promise Me Tomorrow

(YA Contemporary)

Aileron Books

donnajostone.com

© 2024 Donna Jo Stone

All rights reserved. No portion of this book may be reproduced or transmitted in any form, by any electronic or mechanical means, including photocopying, recording, or by any information retrieval and storage system without written permission from the publisher.

*First Edition* September 6, 2024

Ebook ASIN: B0D7ST3SD4
Print ISBN: 9781963387056

Cover Art by Ashely Winter

This is a work of historical fiction. Names, characters, and incidents depicted in this book are products of the author's imagination, or are used in a fictitious manner. Any resemblances to actual persons, living or dead, are purely coincidental. Bible verses are taken from KJV.

# Dedication

Dedicated to my mother, a girl from England who married an American and raised a family in the US.

I miss you.

Made in United States
Orlando, FL
06 September 2024